BEDDING
the Baby Daddy

Bedding The Bachelors Book 9

by
VIRNA DEPAUL

Bedding The Baby Daddy
Copyright © 2017 by Virna DePaul

BEDDING THE BABY DADDY

Wealthy Dante Callaghan certainly earned his reputation as a playboy, but now that he's caring for his younger sister, he's happily exchanged night clubs and one-night-stands for Disney movies and play dates. Moreover, for the first time in his life, he's interested in committing to one special woman. Unfortunately, Aurora LeMonde doesn't want anything to do with him.

Despite her undeniable attraction to Dante, Aurora has been in love with her boss Gio Esposito for years. When she learns Gio's heart belongs to someone else, Aurora's not strong enough to turn down the distraction Dante offers. With his permission, she'll use him. She'll do everything to him that she ever dreamed of doing to Gio. Only once Dante touches her, Aurora's plans deteriorate—Dante's all she can think of, and soon she realizes he's the only man to ever truly touch her heart.

When Aurora discovers she's pregnant with Dante's baby, will she trust that her child's father is also the man of her dreams? And will Dante stop settling for a piece of Aurora and finally claim all of her, body and soul?

1

Aurora LeMonde smiled serenely at each guest who passed her, determined to exude confidence and calm at her company's latest fundraising gala even though she felt like she'd swallowed razor blades. She commanded herself not to do it. Not to torture herself. Not to look at him—at *them*—again. Unfortunately, as was too often the case where her boss, Giovanni Esposito, was concerned, Aurora's self-control was nil. Within seconds, she sought him out, spotting him across the room looking like Italian sin in a perfectly tailored suit. He didn't glance her way, his complete attention focused on the redhead by his side.

Whether he knew it or not, Gio was looking down at the love of his life.

Aurora's eyes threatened to fill, her throat closed and everything behind her eyebrows tightened. With the ease of practice, however, she took a deep breath and swallowed her feelings down.

She'd worked for Gio for five years. Lived and

breathed him. Loved him hard and quiet.

Convinced herself that at some point, the Universe's cosmic puzzle pieces would fall into place and Gio would walk past her office, see her in the right pencil skirt in the right lighting with the right amount of hair tumbling over her shoulder, and he'd just suddenly… requite.

But she'd missed her chance. Or maybe she'd never had a chance at all. Because all along, a lovely redheaded woman had been living and breathing, and now Gio was looking at her like *that*. As if he'd only just started to exist when she showed up.

So really, Aurora had never had a chance. Not for his heart. Because that look on his face? That was the look of Destiny.

On impulse, Aurora snagged a glass of champagne from a passing waiter and drank the liquid down. Maybe she hadn't had a chance at his heart, but damn, it sure would have been nice to sleep with him a time or two. Something to remember fondly in the old folk's home where she would inevitably die alone.

Not that she was feeling bitter or anything.

She scanned the people around her. She knew most of them, Gio's clients, business associates or friends. There they went, smiling and friendly, some of them gazing at her with warm familiarity, but none of them truly knew her. None of them knew that on the inside she was holding her knees and rocking in a corner. Or that she would leave here and climb into bed alone, just as she always did. She hadn't dated in years. Even flirting with a man had made her feel disloyal to Gio.

She couldn't help but chuckle mirthlessly into her champagne at that one.

She'd been faithful to a man who'd seen her as a sister, a friend, a colleague.

Faithful to a man who'd touched her but never *touched* her. She'd made too much of the occasional tap on the shoulder, or hand to help her into a cab, or a few, glorious times, a victory hug when something had gone right for the firm.

Oh how pathetically she'd burned those moments into her brain.

Aurora took another gulp of champagne and told herself that she only had to give it twenty more minutes here before she could escape. This was a fundraiser for lung cancer research, and many of their clients had donated generously to the cause. There were heavy hitters in attendance, including Los Angeles billionaires Jamie Whitcomb and Eric Davenport, who'd flown in from Montana and his self-imposed exile specifically for this event. She needed to put on a good face and mingle, even if her heart was breaking.

She set her empty champagne glass on a side tray and turned to face the music. Unfortunately, she came face-to-face with George Mills Jr., the son of their oldest client. George was one of the slimiest men Aurora had ever had the misfortune to meet, and she'd had to put up with his leering advances for years. Although she'd been quite clear in her disinterest, he'd shown no signs of giving up the pursuit.

His persistence was rivaled only by one other man's, a business colleague who'd made his interest in Aurora very clear, as well. Only *that* man was far from slimy.

A perpetual, incorrigible suitor.

Infuriatingly confident.

Exceedingly handsome.

Out-of-this-world sexy.

Yes, Dante Callaghan was all of those things.

But Aurora hadn't been interested in the notorious playboy when she'd first met him four years ago. And despite the way he'd managed to steal into her dreams on more than one occasion, she still wasn't interested. As far as she'd been concerned, Gio had been the man for her. Now she had to accept they weren't meant to be, but oh how she wished she didn't have to do it in George Jr.'s company.

"Refill, Ms. LeMonde?" he asked, shoving a champagne glass in her hands before she even had a chance to answer.

She took it, but no way in hell was she ever going to drink something George Jr. gave her.

He leered at her, his eyes barely making it above her neckline. Aurora was tall, and at 5'10" she had a perfect view of the pink half-dollar at the crown of George Jr.'s head.

Finally, his beady eyes made it up to her face. "You having a good time?"

What did he expect her to say? It was her company

that was throwing the fundraiser, after all.

"Of course," she answered smoothly. "It's a wonderful event. Is your father here? I'd love to see him."

It was true. George Sr. was a trusted client. Honest, fair, and genuinely personable. How he'd ever spawned George Jr. was a complete mystery to Aurora. She peered down at the little man with a moment's worth of speculation.

He jumped at her momentary attention like a man trying to snatch a salmon out of the river with his bare hands. "He had other plans tonight, unfortunately. Have you given any more thought to my offer?"

Across the room, the woman at Gio's side threw her head back and laughed at something he whispered in her ear. Aurora's stomach tightened. Oh god. She'd never seen Gio whisper in someone's ear. Christ. Christ on a fucking cracker. Aurora felt herself spin away from time and place for a moment. It had been a good laugh too. Nothing put upon or manufactured about it. As much as she hated to admit it, Aurora was starting to think that in different circumstances she might actually like Gio's woman. That thought merely made her stomach clench even tighter.

Aurora tried to focus on George Jr.'s pinched little face. His eyes zipped up from her chest the second he realized she was looking at him again.

Aurora bit down her irritation. That kind of thing had been happening to her since she was about fifteen years old. In so many ways, men were a simple and predictable species. "I'm sorry, what were you saying, Mr. Mills?"

Something flared in George Jr.'s eyes when she referred to him so formally and it made Aurora want to puke. She never in a million years wanted to know what thought had put that lecherous look on his face.

"I was asking if you'd given my offer any more thought. You remember? I talked to you about it when we ran into one another on New Years? My beach house?"

Oh yes. The beach house. The little twerp had had the nerve to invite her, cold turkey, to a private weekend at his beach house in Malibu. Just the two of them.

"Funny," Aurora couldn't quite bite back the retort. "I thought that was more of a proposition than an offer."

George Jr.'s cheeks instantly went bright red. "I merely wanted to—"

"See if Ms. LeMonde could be enticed by your daddy's money?"

The deep voice came from behind her and so did the large, warm hand at the small of her back. Everything in Aurora's body tightened.

Great. Just what she needed right now.

Dante fucking Callaghan. She was so not in the mood for his oxygen sucking presence. Even so, she had to stop herself from instinctively turning around to admire how stunning he was sure to look. His light brown hair was short but somehow always looked a little bit messy and his sharp face was always shadowed and his blue eyes were always lit with an inner fire that made her feel warm when she stared into them too long. Dante wasn't loud or obnoxious, but he was enormous and commanding. Filling every room with his broad shoulders, all-seeing eyes, and constantly half-amused grin.

George Jr. sputtered and turned even redder than before. Dante was still standing just behind her, but she could practically feel his barely restrained amusement. She looked at her hands as one of his big paws plucked her untouched champagne away from her and replaced it with a fresh one.

Finally, he stepped in front of her, and Aurora was immediately swallowed up in the endless night sky of his deep blue eyes. Damn those gorgeous eyes. They just had to be attached to one of the most irritatingly sexy men in history.

"I was insinuating nothing of the sort, Aurora!" George Jr. insisted, puffing up like a balloon. "If you must know, Callaghan, I was simply—"

"Do yourself a favor and quit while you're ahead, Junior," Dante said, taking a casual sip of his drink and sliding even closer to Aurora.

Aurora barely stopped herself from choking on the champagne she was swallowing. She'd always known that Dante was irreverent, but George Mills Jr. was the son of one of the most influential men in the city. As one of the best financial analysts in the business, Dante often teamed up with Gio on projects, which was the reason Aurora saw him so often.

Too often for her comfort.

George Jr., apparently choosing to retreat, at least for now, stiffly nodded in Aurora's general direction and turned on his heel.

Somehow she managed to bite back her smile of gratitude. "Honestly, Dante," Aurora said, looking at him admonishingly.

"What?" He raised his hands in an almost childlike gesture. "He was being a dick, so I made him feel like a dick. What's the harm in that?"

Aurora rolled her eyes and put a few more inches of space between them. "The harm is that he's the son of our biggest client."

Suddenly feeling as if she couldn't stand another minute of this—work obligations be damned—Aurora set her glass down and started to walk away.

"Oh, come on, LeMonde, you know that Mills isn't going anywhere, no matter how many times Junior gets his feelings hurt. He swears by you and Gio."

"That may be true," she retorted immediately, the words hot on her tongue and surprisingly easy to let loose. After what felt like a lifetime of repressing the things she wanted to say at the moment she wanted to say them, it was nice to be able to speak to someone with a little spice. "But what's the point in testing the theory? It's just like you to act without thinking and then disappear, no cares for the person who's going to have to clean up your mess!"

"What mess?" he demanded, getting in front of her and stopping her progress. "What person?"

Aurora pulled up short and longed to press her hands to her hips. But she knew exactly what that would look like. Two people fighting on the edge of a work party. As such, she folded her hands carefully in front of her and gritted her teeth into what she hoped would look like a polite smile to anyone watching from afar.

"George Jr.'s bruised little ego is the mess I'm referring to. And *I'm* going to be the one who has to nurse it back to health next time he comes by the office. All while desperately attempting to avoid his..." Hands? Eyes? Breath? Each option was equally abhorrent so Aurora gave up choosing. "Everything!"

Dante's jaw clenched before it relaxed and he sighed. "You're right," he said, cupping her elbow as she tried to step around him. "I shouldn't have butted in like that. I just wanted him to put his damn eyes back in his head where they belong."

"That makes two of us," Aurora conceded. She eyed him suspiciously. Why was he being so nice? So... human. Usually this far into an interaction he would have asked her out twice already. Instead, here he was, actually looking her in the eye and treating her like he understood her problems.

And then his eyes dropped to her breasts.

"He's lucky I didn't stitch his eyes closed for looking at you the way he was, Jessica."

Aurora's mouth dropped open. Aaand the asshole was back. Scanning her body with those deep blue eyes and calling her by the wrong name.

"Are you fucking kidding me, Callaghan?" Her professional veneer burned to a crisp as her temper spiked. She took a step forward into his space and planted a finger on his broad chest. Aurora was tall in her heels, pushing six feet, but he still towered over her. His sinful mouth quirked in a smile and his dark hair fell over his brow. "We work together for four years, you hitting on me like a frat boy the *entire* time, and now you can't even get my name right? Jesus. What am I, a magnet for fuck boys?"

She threw her hands up, as if asking that question of the cosmos itself, and Dante easily reached up, snatched her hand out of the air and laced his fingers through hers.

"I know your name, Aurora. Trust me. I've grunted it into my pillow enough times after business meetings with you."

Aurora schooled her face into a neutral expression, refusing to give him the satisfaction of her shock. "You're an absolute pig, Callaghan."

"No," he corrected, holding her hand tight when she tried to tug it free and tracing a circle on the inside of her wrist with his thumb. "I'm a man. And you're the most beautiful woman in the room no matter which room it is."

For a moment, his words caused pleasure to ripple through her, but she reminded herself that's all they were: pretty words being uttered by a master of seduction. She smirked and tugged at her hand again. "Yet you can't seem to remember my name."

"I only called you Jessica because you look like Jessica Rabbit in this dress."

Aurora instantly regretted the surprised laughter that bubbled up out of her. She bit it back, ignoring the pleased look on his face. Aurora looked down at her red floor-length gown. It was pretty sexy, she supposed. But it was far classier than it was sex bomb. "I do not."

"You do too. Trust me, when I saw you from across the room my eyes did the cartoon *awooooga* thing." He used his hands to show his eyes bursting out of his head.

Aurora bit back another burst of laughter, crossed her arms and tucked her hands safely away from him. "Well. That sounds like your problem, not mine. Now, if you'll excuse me, I have clients to speak with."

She knew she was being snooty. And the Esposito Group *did* often partner with Dante's firm on larger projects, but honestly, if her behavior lost them the partnership, part of her would be relieved to not be around him as often. He was just so irritating. So big and direct. So frustratingly gorgeous and tempting, even if it was all a game to him.

Thankfully, she managed to walk away without Dante trying to stop her again. She told herself she wasn't disappointed. And in truth, she wasn't terribly surprised. Dante was a flirt, and he'd made it clear on more than one occasion how badly he wanted her, at least physically. But he never pushed too far. Moreover, he was always scrupulously professional in any meeting they had.

She didn't mind the attention he paid her. Just like she didn't mind his eyes on her ass as she strode away. She just couldn't give in to him—even when she was devastated by the knowledge that Gio was at this very moment with the redheaded woman of his dreams.

Aurora melted into the crowd and immediately let

herself get sucked into a conversation. Ten more minutes and she was out of here.

With nothing but a weekend of eating ice cream and thinking about Gio. Oh joy.

She was just ducking away from the party, time obligations completely fulfilled, when a hand tapped her shoulder.

Aurora schooled her face into a friendly expression and turned right into Gio's chest.

"Leaving so soon?" he asked in a friendly way, no censure in his tone at all.

He looked happy, Aurora realized with both a sinking and a rising in her gut. She wanted him to be happy. She was just still reeling from the fact that he was happy with another woman.

"Headache," she said, knowing full well she was taking the coward's way out.

Gio's eyes instantly narrowed in concern. "Are you sick?"

"No, no," she hurried, feeling bad for lying. "Just a little tired is all."

"Well, do you have it in you to make small talk for five more minutes? There's someone I've been wanting you to meet."

"Sure," Aurora said weakly, knowing full well who he wanted her to meet. Her chest tightened and her pulse kicked up like a storm off the water. She followed Gio in a daze through the crowd.

And then, there she was, the lovely redheaded woman.

Standing right there. Looking perfect and petite and saying something to Aurora that she could barely hear over the roaring in her own ears.

Aurora shook hands, nodded her head, laughed politely in the right places. And then three minutes later she was drifting away from them, having said her goodnights.

She found herself in the back hallway toward the coat check, staring at a blank spot in the air. What the hell had just happened? She'd just met the woman that Gio was going to take home and make love to tonight. More than that, she'd just met Gio's future wife. She just knew it. She felt it in her bones. She was no psychic, not like her mother, but that didn't mean she didn't have above-average intuition.

Aurora felt a nauseous panic race through her. Gio's woman was so pretty. Sweet and kind. Rose. The prettiest flower there was.

"Aurora?"

She gritted her teeth at the gravelly voice that instantly sent shivers down her spine.

"What?" she couldn't help herself from snapping as she turned and faced Dante in the dim light of the back hallway.

He raised his hands in surrender. "I didn't come back here to irritate you. Are you alright? You look like you've seen a ghost."

Aurora studied him in the bluish light, her blurry vision suddenly painfully clear. The noise of the party faded away as shadows cut across his face, accenting his sharp jaw, bottomless blue eyes, and dark brows. He was so big he damn near took up the entire hallway. He was so big, in fact, that he made Aurora feel small. Which was saying something, because she'd never been delicate or petite, even as a child.

The scent of him—soap and detergent and whiskey—drifted toward her in the small space and her pulse started racing. In that moment, for the first time ever, she willingly opened herself up to the attraction he made her feel and considered the possibilities…

She cocked her head to one side, studying him, and his brow furrowed like he was trying to figure out her mood.

A thought was uncurling inside her. A dangerous thought. But an interesting one nonetheless. Why should Gio be the only one getting busy tonight? She could damn well do with some good old fashioned sweaty sin. It had been long enough.

And maybe it would help. But only if it was hot. She needed something hot enough to burn these feelings of jealousy and loss right out of her.

So, the question was whether or not Dante Callaghan would fumble in the end zone or if he'd give it to her right. Her eyes dropped to his large hands tucked halfway into his pants pockets. They moved to the confident width of his shoulders. And lastly, they focused on the noticeable bulge behind his zipper.

Her eyebrows raised. Well, even if he was terrible in

bed, she could work with that. "Was it all talk?" she asked him, her voice husky and seductive even to her own ears.

He frowned and cocked a brow. "Excuse me?"

She took a step toward him. "All the pretty words you've had for me over the years. Was it talk? Were you ever going to do something about it?"

Dante's eyes immediately narrowed in comprehension while the rest of him remained perfectly still. "Are you asking me to do something about it?"

Aurora slowly shrugged one shoulder, feeling the fabric of her dress tighten around her breasts. She was feeling reckless and needy and like her soul might just dry up tonight if she didn't feed it something. And right now, what she wanted to feed it most was Dante Callaghan.

"For some reason, yes. I am. So what do you say?"

2

Dante was about half a second away from dropping to his knees and thanking the ever-loving universe that he'd talked himself into coming to this party tonight. Even as he'd driven over here, he'd known it was going to be just another exercise in futility. He'd get to see Aurora, flirt with her for as long as she could possibly stand his presence, and then he'd leave. He knew the routine at this point. He'd been doing it for four years.

She was the one woman that he couldn't get out of his head. She'd steadily rejected him with exactly zero holes in her armor and it wasn't difficult to guess why. It wasn't because she wasn't attracted to him—he saw the flare of desire in her eyes even when she tried to hide it. And it wasn't because she found him unlikable or dull—another thing she was bad at hiding was the smile she couldn't quite bite back at times. He suspected Aurora's refusal to entertain any possibility of dating Dante was because of his reputation for being a ladies man. God knows he'd earned it. But most of that was in his past. Once his little sister, Michelle, had come to live with him, he hadn't exactly been in a position to carry on as he had been. And the truth was, the lifestyle had already started to bore him. Now, there were plenty of nights when Dante found himself kicked back, watching Inside Out with a little girl at home. Or, unfortunately, sometimes watching it with her in a hospital, since Michelle had a rare blood disease called Von Willebrand disease, which required quite a few trips to the doctor's office and even a live-in nurse at times. He found a woman when he needed one, but it wasn't often. His life was a far cry from the clubs and bars that he used to frequent.

But he didn't miss his old life much at all.

He did, however, miss Aurora when they were apart. And that was just his bad luck.

He wasn't pining for her, wasn't in love. He didn't know her well enough to love her. But he knew they would be good together if she ever gave him a shot. When his aunt had invited Michelle to stay the night with her tonight, Dante had thought, what the hell? Why not go and get rejected by Aurora again.

Funny how getting rejected by her was far more appealing to him than dating any other woman.

Now here Aurora was, the dim light of the hallway wrapped around her like a blanket, her huge, gorgeous hazel eyes blinking up at him through the dark, the red silk dress she wore making Dante certain she'd taste like cherries.

All the blood in his body rushed south at the exact same time his breath left his chest. He felt as if he were standing on the edge of a cliff, trying to time the ocean waves so he wouldn't hit the shore when he took the leap of his life.

His body screamed for him to close the distance between them. It was two steps. They'd stood two steps apart plenty of times in his life. But tonight, for some reason, it was two steps with the knowledge that she wanted him *and* was finally ready to do something about it.

He found himself leaning toward her but then his brain wrapped a leash around his dick and yanked himself backward. The phrase *for some reason* echoed in his head as he crossed his arms over his chest and surveyed Aurora. He hadn't been lying when he'd told her that she was the most beautiful woman in any room she ever walked into. Dante often found himself with a racing heart and sweaty palms when he sat across from her at business meetings.

And here she was, those gorgeous, plump lips parted, just a peek of her pearly teeth. Her eyes looking up at him like, *touch me.* But there was something else there, too.

For some reason, she'd said. For some reason she was considering being with him.

"Mind if I ask what the hell happened to change your mind after four years of turning me down flat?" He heard the words leave his mouth and could barely even believe it. Why the holy fuck was he questioning her?

Aurora's expression immediately flattened. Her hand

came to her lush hip as she tossed her mane of glossy blonde hair back over one shoulder. "Look, Callaghan. Either you want me or you don't. This offer expires in about five seconds."

Welp. He'd tried. And when she put it like *that*…

Dante's body yanked the leash back away from his brain and he closed the distance between them in one giant step. He had her backed up against the wall, her eyes wide, and her arms pinned up over her head in two seconds flat.

The heat kicking off of her skin was insane. Almost feverish. She was searing him even through their clothes. He circled her wrists in one of his hands and the other one trailed down the outside of one of her pinned arms. His hand stuttered as he dragged it down her side. Jesus. Her skin was literally softer than the silk of her dress.

Dante leaned forward, crowding her. He was deeply obliged to see heat flare in her eyes, to feel her panting breath wash over him. His eyes dropped to her lips, and then he was leaning forward, wanting nothing more than to suck on that lower lip that had haunted him for half a decade.

Aurora quickly turned her head to one side, giving him access to her long, sleek neck, but avoiding his mouth.

It wasn't lost on Dante. So that's how it was going to be, huh? No affection at all? Not even kissing. Well, that was fine by him. He'd take however much he could get. That was the story of his life, actually. And he didn't see why tonight would be any different.

He ran his nose from her collarbone up to her ear. Her

smell was completely natural, bare. Nothing manufactured or sprayed on. It was just woman, earthy, raw, somehow delicate, like a leaf unfurling in the first weeks of May.

He couldn't restrain the groan that her scent tore out of his throat. The sound of it was desperate, even to his own ears. Time to get things moving. He took a step back from her and her eyes fluttered open in surprise.

"My car's out front."

He started to tug her toward the coat check but she stumbled behind him, yanking at his hand.

"Wait," she said and then tugged that fucking lip between her white teeth. "There's a perfectly good coat closet right here."

She looked up at him from beneath her thick fringe of lashes, her dark eyes like a black hole sucking him in. Dante considered the option for all of two seconds before he dismissed it.

"I'm not going to fuck you within 100 feet of George fucking Junior."

Aurora laughed, obviously surprised by his words. He turned just in time to see the light of humor dance over her face. It made his chest tight to see it.

"Besides," he continued. "Coat closets are for a fast fuck with clothes on. If we're doing this, Aurora, I'm not going to be interrupted while somebody looks for their other glove. Fuck no." He stepped back and took her chin in his hand, staring her right in the eyes. "If we're doing this, it's not going to be some discreet close-your-eyes-and-think-of-England. If we're doing this, then it's going to be absolutely indecent. You and me. Destroying each other. Understood?"

He thought, for one terrifying second, that his words had been too much. That he'd lost her. But then her little, pink tongue peeked out to wet her lip and she nodded.

"My coat is that one there," she whispered, pointing.

Dante reached back and ripped it off the hanger. He held it up for her to slip into and for the first time in living memory, didn't inwardly groan when she covered up her body in a coat. Because now that he knew he was going to see the rest of her, he wanted her to be zipped up throat to ankle. No other man got to look at her tonight. Tonight she was all his.

She quickly did the buttons on her coat and looked up at him. "Get your car. I'll meet you outside."

Something twisted in his stomach; she didn't want to be seen leaving with him. For some reason, it annoyed the shit out of him. He was usually a very live-and-let-live sort of guy. Whatever made it work for a woman, he was game for. But it had been a long time since a woman straight up didn't want to be seen with him. These days he was used to having the opposite problem. He was used to women wanting to be seen everywhere with him.

Considering he'd basically been begging for this for four years, Dante was not going to question or push her any further. Still... He couldn't just leave like this either. The thin string that was pulling them both along tonight was liable to snap if he left her side.

So Dante stepped forward again and took her chin in

his hand. He let his thumb grip her tightly while the rest of his fingers fanned out softly along her jaw. "Fine. But you are not going to talk to anyone else. You're not going to look at your phone. You're not going to do anything but imagine what it'll feel like to have me ten inches deep. You understand?"

Her eyes widened and he could have sworn she was pressing her legs together beneath her dress. Time for the final nail in the coffin. "And if you're not outside in four minutes, I will come back in here and drag you out over my shoulder. In front of anyone and everyone. Understood?"

Aurora nodded and she looked so sincere, so honest, so unbelievably turned on, that Dante felt his chest get tight again. He turned away from her, jogging out toward his car. He didn't care if that looked overeager. He didn't give a flying fuck. All he cared about was getting the hell away from this party and getting a second of time alone with her.

He pulled his Mercedes up to the curb in two minutes and he was deeply pleased when she immediately came walking out. If he wasn't mistaken, she looked a little nervous, a little turned on, and a little sad. Funky combination. Dante wanted nothing more than to make this night a hell of a lot simpler for her. All he wanted was to make her feel good as hell.

The light spring breeze played with the ends of her golden hair and made Dante's fingers itch to do the same thing. She slid into the passenger seat as he pulled smoothly from the curb.

"Rihanna?" she asked, a small smile playing on her full lips.

"Girl's got pipes," Dante said, cracking the windows just a bit. He wanted her hair to float around again.

She laughed, just a small, husky note. And it made Dante rock hard against his zipper. He'd made her laugh twice tonight and it was doing something to him. He'd never heard her laugh before. She was always so serious, so professional, so perfect. He was deeply looking forward to getting her messy.

"Can I ask you a question?"

Her eyes shuttered immediately. "Maybe."

Dante cleared his throat and turned to look at her bathed in the red light of the intersection. He didn't want to miss her reaction. "What's a fuck boy?"

He was not disappointed. Aurora threw her head back and laughed with abandon. "Excuse me?"

He grinned at her. "You said you were a magnet for fuck boys. What did you mean?"

"It's something us younger folks say."

"Rude. I can't be that much older than you, can I?"

"What're you, forty?"

"Ouch. Thirty-eight."

"You've got a decade on me."

She was younger than he'd thought, but as he looked at her, a ghost of a smile on her lips, the swell of her breasts pushing against her thin coat, Dante didn't give a flying fuck how old she was long as she was legal. He

23

shrugged. "So what did you mean?"

Aurora tilted her head, thinking. "Well, it has a few meanings. But it's somebody who only wants to fuck. Who'll do whatever he can to make it happen. And then he disappears. But he kind of messes with your head in the process."

Wow. Christ. "You said I was a fuck boy when you thought I'd called you 'Jessica'."

She shrugged. "Well, maybe you're a fuck *man*."

He eyed her, one hand on the wheel. "You think I'm being a fuck boy right now?"

Aurora studied him, turning in her seat to face him. He got the strange feeling that she was looking straight through him, at some part of him that even he didn't know about, and it was pumping blood straight to his cock, even as he waited for her answer.

"No. I don't think you're messing with my head."

"I'm not," he responded instantly. "I won't."

She shrugged before turning back to face the road.

"Do you live far?" Aurora asked, and then for some reason, her cheeks went a little pink and she cast her eyes down. "Um, I mean, is wherever we're going far?"

She thought he was taking her to a hotel? Hell to the absolute no. "I live about five minutes from here. And my bed is about twenty seconds beyond that."

She looked up at him and he thought he detected relief in her gaze.

"Alright."

Some of the intensity from the hallway had started to

ebb away from them. In its absence, Dante was starting to sense her nervousness, her vague unease. Well, fuck that. The only thing she was going to feel tonight was good, if he had anything to do with it. Wanting to distract her from whatever thoughts were haunting her, Dante took her hand and brought it up to his mouth.

He kissed her palm, just once, almost absentmindedly, before he nipped his way down her wrist. His eyes on the road, all he could do was listen to the sweet little gasping sound she made.

"Aurora, sweetheart, if you're particularly attached to that dress, you better start unzipping it now, because it's not going to last long once we get through my front door."

Once again, she made a little gasping noise that had him gripping the steering wheel hard in order to keep the car on the road.

She pulled her wrist out of his grip and then Dante thanked god for the red light that allowed him to turn and stare as she flicked one button after another on her coat. Her skin was golden, even in the dim light of the car and the crimson of her dress was muted to a deep blood red.

Her coat fell away and he watched in hypnotized slow motion as her hands went around to the side of her dress.

Dante cursed as the car behind them honked. He stepped on the gas and turned onto a side road. If she was stripping down, he did not want some teenager on his way home from his shift at a gas station able to peek in and see. He turned down another and another side road, officially taking the long way home, but he didn't care. The street lights fell away and the houses gave way to trees. There weren't any headlights on the road but theirs.

Dante's heart tried to crawl up his throat as he watched her zip the side of the dress down. He could feel her eyes on his face but he was looking nowhere but at her breasts as she let the top of her dress fall away and her red lace bra was revealed.

Holy shit, she was going to kill him. He felt his blood pressure rise up and he licked his lips. Her breasts, large and golden and spilling over the confines of her bra, were panting up and down with her breath.

He reached out with one of his hands, unable to keep from touching her, but she moved at the same time and he only grazed her warm shoulder with the backs of his knuckles. Dante would have complained but she was moving toward him. She stretched her seatbelt and leaned over the center console. He felt her breath on his neck and then those soft, plump lips against his throat. Just the sweetest little press.

Her breasts pushed against his arm and Dante tightened his grip on the steering wheel. He wasn't going to be able to touch her tonight if he crashed the car. So he laser-focused his eyes before him and took a deep breath. And then she opened her mouth, just the tiniest bit, and he felt her tongue trace over him.

She was tasting him?

Yeah. The driving part of the night was over. Dante pulled the car off the side of the road.

Aurora instantly pulled back from him, confused. But

he'd had enough. Couldn't take it another second. He pushed his seat all the way back from the steering wheel, unbuckled his seat belt and then hers, and then grabbed her around the waist, dragging her into his lap.

She gasped, gripping him around the neck to steady herself. Dante had to lean back and look at her. Her dress pooled at her waist, preventing him from seeing her panties and he couldn't abide it. He gently yanked the soft fabric up over her head and tossed it into the passenger seat.

Holy god. There she was. Straddling him, raised up on her knees, her hair spilling over her shoulders. Fragrant and tumbling and adorning her body like it was jewelry. Her lace bra matched her red lace underwear and Dante's mouth went completely dry.

"Jesus god," he muttered, tracing his hands up her perfect, tight little waist. His hands paused over her ribs, framing her lush breasts. Where to start? He reached up to kiss her and again she turned her head, softening the rejection by offering her neck to him.

The same frustration he'd felt before opened up inside of him. But he couldn't let it ruin the moment. He dropped his head to her pulse point and kissed her there like he would her mouth.

Aurora's body tightened and liquefied all at once. He grinned against her skin when she moaned, deep in her throat. He skimmed his hand over her back, strong and sure, straight to her ass. And then he pulled her right down over him. Her heat landed over the zipper of his pants and she let out a helpless, desperate sound.

Dante broke away from her neck and landed his forehead against her collarbones. He stared down at her breasts as one of his hands played with the seam of her panties at her ass.

"Damn you for ruining red lace for me, Aurora," he muttered.

"What?"

"I fucking love red lace. But no one will ever look this good in red lace again. It's ruined for me."

Aurora started to chuckle but it ended on a moan when his tongue licked the swell of her breast, dipping under the lace of her bra.

The heat of her pussy was burning him, even through their clothing, and Dante couldn't help but push upward.

Aurora moaned and her head fell back. Dante felt the tips of her hair tickle his knees. He couldn't help himself, with her all laid out like that for him. He pushed up with his hips again, driving his hard cock against her.

"Never thought I'd fuck you in a car," he murmured, anchoring his hands at her hips and thrusting up again. His fingers dug into her ass as he pressed her down onto himself. One of his thumbs tucked under the lace of her panties and inched toward her core.

"Where'd you think about it being?" Aurora asked breathlessly, lifting her head and eyeing him with those dark eyes.

"Everywhere. I hoped it would be in your office. Over your desk. You bent forward. One of your tight little skirts up around your waist. I wouldn't even care about closing the fucking door."

Aurora moaned and pressed her hips forward again. She liked that. Well, that was easy. He could do that all night long.

He slipped his whole hand into her underwear now, tracing circles on the smooth skin just above her pussy.

"I pictured fucking you in the back of the club where we ran into each other last year. Remember that? The dark room, flashing lights. You were wearing that snug little dress." She nodded her head, showing she remembered. He plowed on. "That idiot bartender kept talking to you and I wanted to slam his head into the bar, pick you up and drag you into the bathroom. I would have put your hands on the sink and made you watch in the mirror while I fucked you."

"Yes," she moaned, arching her hips, obviously trying to get his fingers to slide home. He just kept tracing tantalizing circles.

"But one of my favorites is your house."

"What?" her eyelids fluttered open just a little bit as she looked at him through a haze of lust.

"I've dreamed about fucking you at your house."

"You've never been there."
"But I can imagine it. I imagine knocking on your door. You're wearing pajamas. I don't ask. I just come in and pick you up. Slam the door and carry you back to your bedroom. Your room is clean and girly and smells like you. Everything smells like you. When I'm in your room

I'm completely surrounded by you. Your bed has pink sheets. You got pink sheets, Aurora?"

She couldn't answer, only moan, as she gripped his shoulders and worked her hips against him. His thumb, just briefly, teased her clit and she immediately tensed, raising up off him and letting her eyes roll back.

When he took his thumb away again she moaned in disappointment. But he leaned forward to speak right into her ear.

"I fuck you on those pink sheets. So many times that we pass out. The sheets smell like me when I leave so even when I'm gone, you're surrounded by me."

And then he slid a thick finger right into her.

"You're wet. And tight." Dante dropped his head to her shoulder and tightened his eyes closed. God. She might not be able to take him. There was a big size discrepancy here. But she pushed forward on his hand greedily.

Aurora was like a woman possessed and he'd never seen anything more beautiful, more arousing. Her soft fingers dexterously undid the buttons on his shirt, roughly untucking it from his pants. She groaned in frustration when she realized he wore an undershirt underneath. And then he changed the stroke of his fingers inside her and hit a spot that she apparently couldn't multitask through.

Aurora leaned against the steering wheel, her eyes rolling back as one of her hands slammed onto the ceiling of the car and the other threaded into Dante's hair.

Yes. Just yes. She was spread out on his lap, her breasts trapped and straining under her bra and Dante couldn't stand it.

With his one free hand he tugged her bra down and her breasts popped free. He lost the breath right out of his lungs. She was the most beautiful creature he'd ever seen.

"You're fucking Aphrodite."

And then there was no more time for words as he leaned forward and buried his face in her breasts. He suckled, tugged, licked and nipped. He couldn't be stopped. He groaned against her soft, fragrant flesh and burned every second into his brain. Somewhere, dimly, he was aware that she was more than ruining him for red lace, she was ruining him for other women. But how could he dwell on that thought when she was grinding down on his fingers, when her wet channel was starting to tense, when her hands clawed at his shoulders.

He lifted his head from her breasts, wanting, knowing, that he had to watch her face when she came for him for the first time. There was no other option.

Her face was almost painfully beautiful. Blissful, straining, and so, so pleasured.

Dante worked her through the orgasm, one hand curling and petting her from the inside and one hand roughly handling her breasts.

Aurora vibrated, tensed, called out. Her body was a trembling live wire. And then she liquefied against him. She went lax and pliant, falling forward onto him and burying her face in the crook of his neck.

He couldn't help but put his free arm around her, hold her close. He stroked a strong, sure circle over her smooth back and tried desperately to remember how to speak English.

He would buckle her back in and drive her to his house. He could wait until then. He wasn't an animal.

And then her tongue snuck out of her mouth and tasted him again. The hollow at the bottom of his throat. He'd thought she'd be sated, tired, needing a moment to rest. But suddenly she reared back over him and was scrambling for the button on his pants. Her breath was panting, her mouth slack with desire. Her eyes were dark with lust. For him.

He didn't waste time. Lifting his hips, he helped her unbutton his pants and shove them down. His cock sprang free and Aurora's eyes went wide.

"You—you weren't kidding." Her voice was breathy and tinged with something he couldn't quite read.

"About what?" He could barely add two and two right now.

Her eyes slid up from his cock and then back down. "About the ten inches."

"Oh," Dante grinned. "No. I wasn't." He traced a hand up her back and down. "We'll go slow, sweetheart."

Her body was tensing again, even though they were barely touching. She panted and lifted her hips towards him. "I don't think I can."

She was worried about their size difference. He could understand that. She wouldn't be the first woman who'd looked at what he was packing and felt nervous. He laced his fingers through her hair. Leaning forward, he kissed along her neck, wishing she'd let him kiss that pretty mouth. Even if the words were killing him, he ground them out. "We don't have to fuck, baby. There's plenty of other things we can do if you're worried you can't take it."

"No," she pulled away from him, a fierce look on her gorgeous face. "No, I meant I don't think I can go slow."

She pulled that juicy lip between her teeth and rocked against him. He blinked twice, absorbing her words, before he flipped up the center console, grabbed a condom and sheathed himself.

Aurora breathlessly smiled. "Someone's eager."

"Been waiting four years," he growled, sliding her panties down her legs. He helped her out of them, jamming them in the pocket of his pants, and then settled her back on his lap.

Dante swiped a thumb through her heat and couldn't resist sucking her sweetness right off. Sparks flew in his vision as he finally tasted her. He cursed himself that he couldn't have waited until he got her in a bed, because there wasn't enough room in this car to go down on her. But all thoughts of regret disappeared as she lowered herself down on him, the head of his cock sliding into her.

She paused, barely able to take more than an inch. She made a greedy, desperate noise as she tried to sink further, but couldn't.

Immediately, Dante's thumb was on her clit while his other hand went to the back of her neck, drawing her forward. He held his hips completely still while he stroked her and nestled his lips right in her ear.

"That's a good girl. Just like that," he coaxed her. She moaned and pushed her clit forward into his touch and the movement had her taking another inch. "Just work yourself down, little by little, you gorgeous fucking goddess. Good girl."

She moaned again and he could feel her wetness dripping from her all the way down him. He struggled to remain still, refusing to thrust upward until she was ready, but it might have been the hardest thing he'd ever done. Dante gritted his teeth and continued whispering dirty sweet words in her ear. Aurora worked herself down, taking him inch by tortuous inch.

And then she was fully seated on him. She'd taken his entire length. Dante hoped that someday he'd get his vision back. But right now, all he could do was feel. Grit his teeth against the painful, delirious tidal wave of pleasure that was her pussy. She squeezed him like a fist.

A small noise from the back of her throat had his eyes fluttering open and what he saw there stunned him. He'd never seen a sexier expression on a woman's face before. She licked at her bottom lip and Dante couldn't help but thrust his hips up.

He was already as deep as he could possibly go but the added pressure had her head dropping back.

"Oh god," she whispered as she rose up on her knees, almost all the way up off of him, before she pushed back down and swallowed him whole.

"Fuck," he growled. If she did that again, the show was going to be over way too soon. Gripping her lush hips in both hands, Dante lifted her up and slammed her back down. He set a grueling pace. Hard and smooth and everything he'd wanted for years.

Her scent filled the car and Dante's choppy breaths tried to draw it all in. He wanted her to fill his lungs. He could still taste her on his tongue and that was the only thing that was keeping him from jamming his tongue down her throat.

He bounced her on top of him as she moaned and tightened. She allowed him to guide the pace but her hips moved of their own accord. Her movements were sinuous and harsh at the same time. God, she really was a goddess. Made to be worshipped and pleasured.

"I'm going to—" She gasped. "I'm going to—"

"That's right," he growled. "Give it up, gorgeous. Give it to me. All over me."

Her eyes dropped to his as her body started seizing again. A helpless gasp left her lips as he speared up into her, his body drawn to hers as if by magnet. Unable to help himself, Dante leaned up into her, and quick as lightning, drew her bottom lip between his teeth.

It wasn't quite kissing. For a moment, he thought she might pull away. But then her orgasm crested through her, tightening her pussy around his shaft and her fingers at his shoulders. He sucked that lip into his mouth as she screamed her release.

And then she was limp again, leaning against him and unable to do more than take his thick thrusts.

"This fucking car," he growled as his feet struggled

for purchase. He needed more fucking space. He had Aurora Goddamn LeMonde in his arms and on his cock and he couldn't even fuck her the way he wanted. Without giving it another thought, he braced his arm around her waist, flung open the door of the car and stepped out with her.

The night air was crisp and it tightened her nipples immediately. She lifted her head off his shoulders, looking around, confused as to what was going on. But there was no more waiting, no more hesitation. He grabbed his suit coat from the front seat, and strode, with her still taking his entire length, to the hood of the car. He tossed his coat down before laying her over it.

He reared back and burned the image into his brain. The moonlight on her skin, the shadows of leaves dancing over her face, her breasts, pebbled and calling to him. If anyone were to drive past, they'd see exactly what was happening. A lucky son of a bitch fucking a gorgeous woman on the hood of his car. But Dante couldn't bring himself to care. He was beyond logic.

He pushed in, his body screaming for release in this new position.

"Yes," she whispered, her back arching and her hair fanning out all around her.

It was all the encouragement he needed. Dante clamped her legs around his waist and planted a hand on either side of her head. And then he fucked her like an animal. Like an absolute beast. He was aware of her body bearing down on his again. Of her screaming for god. And then, most deliciously, her begging him for more.

He gave it to her, and to himself. Nothing had ever been more right. Hotter or tighter or wetter. When the fire rose up his spine and he knew he was close, Dante fell over her. His hands slid under her back, gripping her by the shoulders and holding her still while he lost himself in her. She grabbed him back, just as tight, as the brightest, darkest, slow-motion high-speed explosion tore away from him and right into her.

3

Six weeks later

Aurora froze as she walked back into her office with the salad she'd just picked up down the street. There were flowers on her desk.

These days there were *always* flowers on her desk.

She put her salad down and picked up the lilies, then glanced at the card, which was once again simply signed "From Dante." With a sigh, she caressed the D in his name with her fingertips before placing the card along with the stack of identical cards in her desk drawer. Then she strode back out to the break room. Gently, she placed the flowers into the vase along with yesterday's roses and the daisies from the day before. The office was running out of vases, and she was running out of patience with Dante Callaghan.

AKA the biggest mistake of her life.

She strode back into her office and shut the door. She just wished she could shut the door against the memories that assaulted her whenever she thought of him. The way he'd rearranged her clothes then set her gently back in the front seat after he'd given her some of the most intense orgasms of her life. How he'd held her hand as he'd driven her to his house. How he'd carried her up to his room like she hadn't weighed a thing.

And how he'd rolled with her, kissed every inch of her, made her scream for hours.

Aurora squeezed her eyes closed and let her head fall back on the door. The image that tortured her, the one that made her feel like she couldn't breathe, was how he'd looked just before she'd snuck out early the next morning. Peaceful and sated and somehow dangerous. It was like watching a lion sleep. She couldn't believe how much of her had wanted to crawl back into bed with him, lick up his stomach and see what happened. But the rest of her, the *sane* part of her, had been screaming for her to get the fuck out of there before he woke up and they had to talk about whatever the hell had happened.

So, she'd snuck out, gotten an uber, and hadn't spoken to him in over six weeks. Unfortunately, the memories of their time together kept playing in her head, even at the most inopportune times. It was playing with her head. Distracting her. Affecting her performance at work. Which was why she was ducking him. She'd made up bullshit excuses to Gio, and he'd taken over all interactions with Dante.

She was hoping that eventually, if she distanced herself from him enough, the memories of their passion would fade and things would go back to the way they'd used to be. Sure, she'd always found him attractive, but she'd convinced herself his arrogance irritated her too much to ever give in to that attraction. She could convince herself of that again.

Dante Callaghan and his magic cock were not on her list of things she was going to spend time or energy on.

Only he wasn't making moving on easy for her, damn him.

After she'd snuck out on him, there'd been radio silence for a few days. Something that had both relieved and, weirdly, disappointed her. But then she'd gotten a text from an unknown number.

Pretty sure that of the two of us, YOU'RE the fuck boy.

She'd tried not to smile. She'd tried not to text back, she really had. But then her fingers were somehow acting without her permission.

Excuse me?

Anything to get me in the sack and then you mess with my head. That's the definition, right?

Aurora wasn't sure whether to laugh or to grimace.

I'm not trying to mess with your head.

That's exactly what a fuck boy would say.

Now she really did laugh. She ignored the pinching in her gut when she typed what she did next.

Not trying to play games, Dante. It was a great night. Let's leave it at that.

It *had* been a great night. Actually, it had been the

best night of her life. But no matter how you sliced the pie, she was in love with Gio. And if she couldn't have him, then she was going to have the second most important thing in her life. Her career.

Not to mention the fact that Dante was a major player. He'd pursued her for a long time, sure. But she was under no misconceptions that she was the only woman he was treating that way. He'd just wanted what he couldn't have. And, according to the rumors, there was very little that Dante couldn't have. She'd heard through Alice, Gio's intern, that Dante had dated no less than six women in their office building. And it was not a big office building. She didn't know what kind of game he was playing with the flowers, but it wasn't one that Aurora planned to get wrapped up in.

He hadn't texted her again or called since that day, but he had sent flowers almost every day for the last six weeks.

It was flattering, she told herself, that was all. That was the reason that the gesture made her heart beat fast. And the flowers were always beautiful. That was why she had a little pinch in her chest every time she took them out of her office and put them in the break room.

She just wished every time Gio happened to see them, he didn't tease her about the smart man trying to win her heart. Every time he said it, Aurora had to swallow the lump in her throat.

He hadn't said anything about it specifically, but Aurora had the distinct impression that things were on the right track with Rose. She could tell that Gio was happier than he'd been in a very long time, and she in turn tried to be happy for him. Unfortunately, thinking of him with Rose depressed her so much that yesterday, when the gigantic delivery of orangey pink roses came, she'd been tempted, for the first time, to text Dante, see what he was doing.

She'd opened up her phone, brought up a blank text to him. She'd managed to stop herself, however. After all, she thought, what would he think when she texted him out of the blue, what was it, six weeks later?

Six weeks, she once again thought.

Wait…

Six. Weeks.

Was it possible?

Aurora scrolled through her phone to her calendar app. Yup. Sure enough. The lung cancer fundraiser had been six weeks ago. And that meant…

Her stomach in one humongous knot, Aurora did some backwards math. She hadn't had her period in *eight weeks*. Which meant that she'd been exactly two weeks into her very regular cycle when she'd slept with Dante. They'd used a condom every time they'd fucked, but they'd fucked *a lot*, and now she'd missed her period…

In a daze, she lowered herself into her desk chair. She took a deep breath, trying to reassure herself. She hadn't been sick, or had headaches, or cramps, or any other physical symptoms of pregnancy. And she'd been upset. Stressed. Sad about Gio. Women skipped periods all the time over stuff like that, right? Right.

One thing was certain, however, she needed to put her mind at ease, and the best way to do that was a pregnancy test. Only when she took a pregnancy test later that night, she still wasn't reassured. Not completely. Like condoms, pregnancy tests weren't 100% effective, especially when it was early in a pregnancy. So the next day, she immediately called her doctor and set up the earliest appointment she could.

Two days later, Aurora was sitting on the papery table of an examination room trying not to freak the hell out.

"Congratulations," Dr. Radnor said to Aurora. She laid a hand on Aurora's shoulder for just a second. "Do you… have someone to share the news with? Maybe help you think about your options?"

"My mother," Aurora answered weakly, both reassured and crushed by the thought. She wasn't alone, sure. But she didn't have a partner.

She couldn't believe it. She'd been so careful. So restrained. Such a good girl for the most part.

Good girl. Dante's voice echoed through her head. It was what he'd said to her as he'd gently guided her down on his cock, encouraged her to take even more.

The one time she really let herself loose she went and got pregnant.

God. What was she going to do?

* * *

Dante sat in Gio's plush office and drummed his fingers on the arm of the leather chair he was kicked back in.

"No, that's exactly what I was thinking, Doug," Gio said into the speakerphone, turning and raising his eyebrow at Dante's drumming fingers.

Dante rolled his eyes but stopped the nervous habit.

He was annoyed with Gio, but really he was lucky the man had his shit together. He was phoning this meeting in. Just like he had with almost everything for the last six weeks. He just couldn't get his head in the game. And the reason for that was sitting in her office not thirty feet away.

Well, he was actually pretty certain she wasn't sitting in her office. Every single time he'd come to Gio's office for a meeting for the last six weeks, she'd mysteriously disappeared. All for apparently good reasons. Lunch with clients. Picking up something from the printers. An out of office meeting.

He knew she was avoiding him. That much was obvious. The six weeks of silence were evidence of that. He internally rolled his eyes at himself. As if he needed any more evidence that she wanted nothing to do with him given she'd snuck out in the middle of the night.

A night that had left Dante irrevocably changed.

She'd run without leaving anything more than her scent on the pillow, which had clung for a week. When the scent had finally disappeared, he'd reached out to her via text. And that was that. She'd made her feelings clear.

He sent the flowers because... well he wasn't exactly

sure why. He wasn't ready to let this shit go. And she hadn't told him to cut it out, so part of him wondered if he was somehow making progress with her.

Who was he kidding? He wasn't making progress with her. He hadn't struck out this hard with a woman since… well, never. It was fucking with his head. That was why he'd agreed to see Grace tonight. She was an old friend in town for a night on business. One who he'd shared a few mutually satisfying nights with. It was an invitation he would have normally jumped on with no reservations whatsoever. Vigorous sex with Grace could be just what the doctor ordered. He needed to get over this crush or whatever the hell it was he felt for Aurora. So why had he felt like he was cheating on Aurora when he'd made the date?

"What the hell is wrong with you?" Gio demanded as he clicked off the phone call and rounded on Dante. "You barely spoke on that phone call. You know that neither of us are going to land this client if you sit there like a complete jack off."

Dante opened his mouth, automatically getting his hackles up, but really, Gio was right. He scraped a hand over his hair. "You're right."

"What?" Gio looked at him like he'd just announced he was joining a nudist colony.

"I said that you're right. I'm off my game right now. Thanks for carrying the phone call."

"Oh," Gio stared at him, perplexed. "Everything alright?"

"Yeah, we uh, don't have to do the whole feelings thing, man."

"Alright." Gio shrugged. "You going to be ready for the meeting next week? If not, it's better if I just do it by myself."

"No, no." Dante rose from his chair. That's the last thing he wanted. To have someone carry him professionally because he'd gotten his fucking feelings hurt by a woman. "I'll be fine. It's just been a fucked up Spring. But it's over now."

"Alright," Gio said again. He opened up his office door and they walked out. "Did Alice give you the specs for the project yet?"

"No, not unless she emailed them while we were in the meeting." Dante took out his phone and checked his email.

"No worries. Aurora has them," Gio said, striding over to her closed office door and swinging it open.

Dante blinked his eyes in surprise. There she was. Standing beside her desk, shuffling papers. Wearing a blue dress and a long silver necklace. A ponytail. Her gorgeous, blonde hair tumbled over her shoulder in a fucking ponytail. God damn it. He had such a weak spot for ponytails.

She blinked right back at him, obviously shocked to see him.

"Dante! I didn't know you were going be in the office today."

If I had, I wouldn't be here. It was the unspoken other

half of her statement.

Dante stepped up beside Gio in her doorway.

"Unexpected conference call with Doug Wexler," Gio replied.

"Oh!" Aurora looked surprised and excited. "Tell me we got the account."

"Not yet. Wexler's dragging his feet. We're going to meet again next week."

Dante was grateful for Gio not mentioning the fact that Doug Wexler was dragging his feet because Dante was so far off his game.

"Do you have the project specs?" Gio continued, apparently blind to the fact that Aurora was looking absolutely anywhere but at Dante. "Dante needs them."

"Oh, sure." She hurried around her desk to the filing cabinet in the corner. Dante couldn't help but watch the way her beautiful body moved with such grace. Like a panther stalking the length of a branch. She dug through a file for a minute before pulling some papers out.

"Mr. Esposito," Alice called from the other room. "I've got a client on the phone for you."

Gio nodded his head to Dante and ducked out of the room, closing the door behind him. And just like that, Dante and Aurora were alone in her office.

She was holding the papers out to him, her eyes wide and shocked. Dante opened his mouth to say something flirty and snarky, but as he crossed the room he saw the papers shake in her hand. And come to think of it, her normally golden skin was looking awfully pale.

"Aurora, are you alright?" he asked, crossing to her.

"Yes. I just… I'm feeling a little faint…"

Her knees buckled and Dante was at her side in less than a second. He gripped her at the waist and then under her knees. Lifted her right off the floor.

"Dante, that's not necessary," she insisted, but she didn't push away from him or stiffen. In fact, she closed and dropped her head to his shoulder for a second. Dante set her gently in her office chair and immediately knelt beside her.

"What's going on? Are you sick?"

"No."

"Have you eaten today?" His heart was beating a mile a minute.

She gestured to an unopened salad on her desk. "I just picked that up a few minutes ago."

Dante grabbed the salad and ripped the top off. "There's no food in this food!"

"What?" She rubbed a hand over her forehead and looked at him in confusion.

"There's like two pieces of lettuce and one olive. What the hell kind of lunch is this? No wonder you're fainting."

A small smile quirked its way out of her lush lips before she wiped her expression clean. "I happen to like my food. And don't worry about the lightheadedness. I just didn't sleep well last night. What are you doing?"

"I'm fanning you with a file, what does it look like?" Dante was irritated and he wasn't sure why. The woman needed a BLT and a beer. That would set her right. But the odds that he could get her to eat any of that were zero. So she was going to have to just sit there and let him fan her.

She swatted at his hand. "Don't be ridiculous, Dante."

"Just hush up and let me take care of you for a second, Aurora."

Her eyes widened as she stared up at him. She worried her bottom lip between her teeth. Her voice was small when she spoke again, confusion and vulnerability warring in her eyes. "That's what you want?"

He set the file down and didn't break eye contact, knowing that they were suddenly talking about so much more than just her fainting spell. "I want anything you're willing to give me. Anything." His response was truthful.

She nodded. The vulnerability didn't leave her eyes. If anything it intensified.

"I...I..."

Holy shit. Was she looking at his mouth? Dante tensed, not believing his fucking luck, as Aurora leaned forward in her chair. Her breath fanned over his face as he closed the distance between them.

But Aurora pulled back, jumping when his phone buzzed in his pocket.

He ignored it.

"Aren't you going to get that?"

"No. I'm more concerned about you right now."

When his phone buzzed again, she raised her eyebrows. "Please get it. I don't want you ignoring business because of me."

Not wanting to argue with her, he withdrew his phone.

"Fine. I'm sure it's nothing. Now stop trying to pretend everything's okay. You're not okay." When his phone buzzed again, he glanced down. Unfortunately, so did Aurora.

The texts were from Grace.

Hey there, stud. Looking forward to tonight. You want to grab a bite? Or do you just want to get down to the good stuff?

Swiftly, he glanced at Aurora, who looked even paler. For a moment, hurt flashed across her expression but then was quickly replaced by a cynical smirk.

Christ. Of all the fucking timing. "Aurora—"

She swiveled in her chair to face her computer. "Thanks for the help, but I'm feeling much better now."

His stomach clenched as he surveyed her somber profile. She didn't look angry, she looked resigned. God. This was all so messed up. She'd given him an opening and then closed it back up all in less than a minute.

"Alright." It was the only thing he could say that wasn't a land mine right now. "Feel better."

When he left, he closed her office door gently, a movement that was in stark contrast to the fury rumbling through him. Fury at himself.

He shouldn't have made a date with Grace. Shouldn't have planned to use one woman to forget another. It was no use.

Aurora was in his head. In his blood. Hell, possibly even in his heart.

And the truth was, he wanted to keep her there.

4

Aurora laid her head on her mother's lap and let the tears come. Her mother had been so calm. Even when she'd explained that she was pregnant, Cedalie LeMonde had opened her arms to her daughter, stroking her hair and holding her tight.

"Ça bon, piti," Cedalie had said over and over in her native Creole tongue. *It's alright, child. It's alright.*

"You're going to be fine," Cedalie said again, working her fingers through Aurora's hair. "I raised you alone and look how well you turned out. And you have so much more than I did."

Aurora turned to look up at her beautiful mother. Beauty ran deep in their family. Even at 50, her mother could have passed for late 30s. She had the same gold skin as Aurora, but her eyes were blue and her features less sharp than her daughter's. Even more than her mother's beauty, however, Aurora hope she'd inherited her strength.

Her mother had been the next best thing to homeless

when she'd given birth to Aurora. Knocked up and broke, no clue who the father was and selling fortunes on a street corner in New Orleans. And after Aurora had been born, Cedalie's rise from the ashes hadn't exactly been meteoric. They'd scraped and scrounged for every penny, every bite of bread. It had been exactly what had encouraged Aurora toward school, school, and more school. Thankfully, she'd convinced her mother to move to Los Angeles with her so that she could keep an eye on her while she was in business school.

Apparently, she should have had her mother keeping a closer eye on *her*.

As if reading her thoughts, her mother cupped her chin and lifted her face so their eyes locked. "You have a job and money and a place to live, Aurora. That's already so much more than you and I started out with. This child is lucky to have a mama like you."

"But what about a papa for my baby?" Aurora cried.

"Eh," Cedalie waved her many-ringed hand through the air. "Who needs that? A man will just complicate the energy in the household."

Cedalie was old school Louisiana Creole. Not voodoo exactly, but she subscribed to a very different school of thought than the average American. Aurora had long ago accepted her mother's view of the world. One filled with auras and energies and spirits. In some cases, her mother had proved to be damn close to psychic. Whatever that meant.

Aurora had inherited some "vision," her razor sharp

intuition a huge part of the reason she'd done so well in the business world. But for the most part, she kept the mystical side of herself confined to moments when she was with her mother.

"I'm not worried about raising the baby without a papa. I'm worried about raising it *with* one."

"What's that, child?"

"The father of the baby. He's…" Aurora trailed off, totally unsure what she even meant to say. "Not the man I love." Even as she said the words, however, she was surprised that when she tried to think of Gio, Dante's visage remained strong. Almost as if it refused to be pushed aside to let another man inside her head.

Or her heart.

"Hmm." Cedalie eyed Aurora shrewdly and stroked one finger over her daughter's eyebrows. "Tell me about the father, then."

"His name is Dante. He's huge. Takes up every room he's ever in."

"He's loud?"

"No. No, not at all. He's just the kind of guy that people pay attention to. He's always looking for the joke. But he's smart. A good businessman. He's not like us, Mama."

"In what way?"

"He's rich. Very rich. And he's used to people doing everything and anything he tells them to. He's very bossy." Aurora blushed and turned away from her mother.

"Would he be a good father?"

"I have absolutely no idea. He has a million women in the bull pen at all times. He's a total player. Been after me for years and one night I just…"

"You just needed to be loved."

Aurora sat up then. "No. No, that's not it at all. I just needed passion."

"And you sure got it, child." Cedalie stood and poured out a cup of the tea that was steeping in a kettle on the kitchen table. She brought it over to Aurora. "That much is clear just from the look on your face."

Aurora blushed further. There was no use lying to her mother, who would know she was lying anyways. "Well. Yes. He's very passionate. Oh god, Mama this is awful, what is in this tea?"

"It's for good fortune. For you and for the baby. Drink up. Passion is a good quality in a partner."

Aurora released a mirthless laugh. "He's never in a million years going to be my partner."

Cedalie sat back, her silver black hair settling over the large purple sweater she wore. She tucked her feet, clad in mismatched socks, underneath herself and looked out the window. "If you keep the baby, you have to tell the father. It's bad energy to keep a man from his offspring."

Aurora swallowed down the bitterness in her throat. "I know."

She knew that her mother's only regret over the way that Aurora was conceived was that Cedalie hadn't been sure who the father was. It had happened during a wilder time. When she wasn't sure of the names of the men she took to bed, and she damn sure wasn't sure how to contact them again.

Cedalie turned back to her daughter. "But you damn well better be sure you have your ducks in a row before you do. You need to know that man inside and out before you tell him."

"What? Why?"

"A man that rich? A man who gets what he wants? There's no telling what he'll do if he does or doesn't want the baby. You need to be ready. Prepared. And you can't prepare if you don't know him."

"You're telling me to get closer to him?" Aurora heard a tinny ringing in her ears. Her heart was leaping, both from nerves and from something else she couldn't quite identify.

"If you're keeping the baby, you owe it to yourself to know this man. If he's someone who will take the baby from you, then you need to have the legalities in order. If he's someone who will try to convince you not to have the baby, then you need to have an escape plan. If he's someone who will want to raise the baby with you, then you'll have to know him well enough to know if you want it. Pregnancy is a vulnerable time. You need to be armed with information. And a good plan."

Aurora's head was spinning. "I thought you were going to tell me to come home and move in with you. Or convince me it was time to move back to New Orleans."

"No, child. You have untied strings with this man. You tie them up. And then we decide where we live."

Aurora tilted her head back on the couch. "And what about Gio?"

"What about him?"

Aurora lifted her head at the dismissive tone in her mother's voice. "I just go on pretending I don't love him?"

Cedalie reached forward, picked up the tea from the coffee table and shoved it back in her daughter's hand. "Time tells, daughter. You feel your feelings and time tells the truth."

* * *

Dante half-heartedly sank a spoon into his portion of ice cream and tried not to wince at the cotton candy flavor in his mouth. He was more of a chocolate chocolate chip sort of guy. But anything for Michelle. She was sitting next to him at the breakfast bar, swinging her socked feet and humming to herself as she worked her way through her half of the carton.

"Dante, I think you need to start doing yoga," she said out of the clear blue.

He blinked at his little sister, his eyes instantly going wide with humor and surprise. "Excuse me?"

"Yeah," she nodded, in that authoritative way of hers. Her messy hair fell in front of her face and for a moment, her eyes, exactly like Dante's, were blocked. She brushed it away. "It's proven to help with stress."

"I'm not stressed."

"Pffft." She rolled her eyes. "Then how come you're

always going running at the butt crack of dawn? You only do that when you're stressed."

He leaned over and brushed the hair out of her eyes himself, chuckling at her choice of words. "I'd say you need a haircut, but you're already seeing too much as it is, kid."

"So I'm right?"

"About the stress or the yoga?"

"The stress."

Dante eyed his sister, her little frame in the too big shirt, her face so much like their father's. It never failed to be like a dagger in the heart when he saw that man staring up at him out of Michelle's face. When he'd taken her in, he'd promised himself that he'd never do anything the way their father would. And what would their father do right now? He'd lie. So Dante scrubbed his hands over his face and tried to think of a way to tell the truth to a way too intuitive ten-year-old.

"Yeah. I'm stressed. I've been messing things up at work lately."

"Why?" She not-so-surreptitiously dug into his half of the ice cream.

"I've been distracted."

"Because of the woman you've been sending flowers to?"

Dante drew his hand away from his eyes and stared at Michelle in complete astonishment. "How did you know about that?"

She shrugged. "The flower place calls the house

number if they can't get you on your cell. Sometimes they have to make substitutes for whatever you've ordered. I always tell them what changes to make."

There were no words. "Is that right?"

She shrugged. "So, who is she?"

He opened his mouth and clapped it closed again. "Her name's Aurora."

"The woman you work with sometimes?"

"Seriously. How do you know all of this?"

Michelle gave him quite the look. "Dante, we live together, I listen when you talk. It's not rocket science. Plus, I met her at an office picnic. Don't you remember?"

"I guess I forgot." He chuckled, slapped her spoon away from his ice cream with his own spoon and took another bite. "So, yeah, I work with her and…" He trailed off. Nowhere to go from there. How to explain this to Michelle? It was too advanced for a ten-year-old.

"And you have a crush on her," Michelle filled in where he couldn't.

"No," he started, and then reconsidered. He didn't think Michelle needed to hear him talk about being obsessed with Aurora. That one night worshipping at the altar of her body had only served to whet his appetite. Yeah, not the kind of conversation a guy has with his ten-year-old sister. "Well. Sure. I've got feelings for her."

"But she doesn't have them for you?"

Dante shook his head. "Doesn't seem like it. But she let me kiss her one time."

That actually wasn't true. She purposefully *hadn't* let

him kiss her. But he wasn't about to explain that she'd let him fuck the lights out of her. Four times. So, kiss it was.

"And now you send her flowers."

"Yep." He eyed her out of the corner of his eye. She'd had a small health episode with her Von Willebrand's earlier in the week. It had required a short hospital stay. But she was looking a lot better now. She had her color back. He glanced at the clock. It was going to be time for her medicine in a few minutes.

"Did you tell her how you feel?" Michelle asked, sneaking one last bite of his ice cream.

"She knows."

"No," Michelle shook her head again. "In school, they say that you have to make sure you actually explain your feelings, or else the other person might not understand. You might think she knows but maybe she doesn't."

He raised an eyebrow at her. "I've been sending her flowers for six weeks. I think she gets the picture."

Michelle shrugged and slid down from the bar stool. "Flowers mean a lot of things. 'I'm sorry', 'Be my wife', 'Go on a date with me', 'Good luck.' Who knows what she thinks you mean."

Dante blinked at her. Michelle might have a point there. "Alright. Maybe you're right." He chucked his spoon in the tub and followed her from the room. "Time for your medicine."

"Yeah, yeah," she grumbled. But it didn't stop her from reaching up and taking his hand. Just like she did when she'd first come to live with him four years ago.

Dante looked down at her head. The kid was growing up, that was for sure. But he was glad she hadn't grown out of some things yet.

5

A week went by and though Aurora was trying to be patient and follow her mother's advice, time still hadn't told Aurora shit. Except that being pregnant kind of sucked. She was irritable, her nipples had started hurting, and to add insult to injury, she was horny as hell.

Aurora couldn't remember a time in her life when she'd been this turned on. All the time. She couldn't stop thinking about her night with Dante. The hottest sex of her life. And that was really bothering her because she was trying desperately to figure out a way to reach out to Dante as a friend.

Her mother had encouraged her to get to know him better before she broke the news to him. And Aurora could definitely see the wisdom in the advice. However, she had no idea how to pull it off.

They had never been friends, even before they'd slept together. And any advance that Aurora made now was sure to be taken as an indicator that she wanted to sleep together again.

Which she totally did. She couldn't deny that. She'd replayed their passionate night together more times than she could count. But she was certain that it was a bad idea to sleep with Dante again. He scrambled her brains when what she needed to be was clearheaded and deliberate. Now more than ever. As her mother had advised, she needed to figure out what kind of man he was.

Besides, it wasn't like her love for her boss had disappeared overnight, simply because Dante had helped ease her pain for one night. Granted, she'd woken up the next day confused over two men instead of one, but it didn't matter. She couldn't have either of them. Not as a lover or a husband.

But whether she liked it or not, Dante might just play another part in her life. The role of father to her child, if he was so inclined.

As she prepared a file to bring into Gio's office, she pondered how to get to know Dante better without winding up in his bed again. Maybe she could find some work-related project to team up with him on. That way she could be in his sphere, observe him, get to know him, but not run the risk of blurring any lines.

Intrigued by the idea, Aurora straightened her emerald green silk blouse and brushed off her charcoal pencil pants. She smoothed her hair back before she left her office. She was no longer trying to attract Gio, but it didn't hurt to look her best.

She strode into his office, holding the file

triumphantly in the air. "Found it!"

"Thank God," Gio said, pushing back from his desk and coming around to stand next to her. "I really didn't want to have to do all that work over again."

"I'm sorry, are you under the impression that you did it the first time?"

Gio grinned. "Ah. My mistake. I wouldn't have wanted *you* to have to do all that work over again."

She laughed. It was just one of the many things she loved about him. He'd never been intimidated by her competence. Even when she'd started here as his executive assistant, he'd recognized her talent immediately. In many ways, he was her mentor. She stared at the side of his face as he surveyed the file. He was just so dang handsome. All black hair and five o'clock shadow and milk chocolate eyes.

"Am I interrupting?"

Dante's voice came from the doorway. His hair was tousled from the wind and he had a messenger bag slung across his chest.

And he was looking at Aurora like he could see right to the heart of her.

* * *

Suddenly everything made sense. Painfully clear sense.

She was in love with Gio.

Dante had daydreamed about seeing that look on her face. Soft and sweet and hopeful. He'd wanted Aurora to look that way at him, and instead she was doing it for Giovanni Esposito.

Damn. He'd been having such a good day too. Michelle's words had inspired him to come clean to Aurora. He was going to lay his cards on the table. And if she didn't pick those cards up? Well, then he was just going to have to be a big boy and move the hell on.

But now, this. What the hell was he supposed to do with this?

"Ah, Dante," Gio said as he looked up, taking a file from Aurora's hand. "Glad you're here. I have a few things I want to go over with you."

"I'll leave you to it." Aurora ducked out of the room, leaving nothing more than a whiff of her scent. It was subtle, light, but it went straight to Dante's head like a shot of whiskey.

Dante sat down and went over the file that Gio had wanted to show him. He surveyed him, taking stock of Giovanni the way a gladiator might take stock of his opponent in the ring.

Sure, Gio was dating a woman named Rose now, but had Dante missed something? Had Gio and Aurora ever slept together? The thought curdled in his stomach like spoiled milk. He swallowed against the insane rage that rose up through his throat.

"Dante, are you even listening?" Gio was looking at him like he was a crazy man right now. What had he just said?

Dante tried to focus on the business at hand, but he

found his mind was still spinning. All he could think about was the fact Aurora was in love with a man who didn't want her. And somehow, that had ended up with her being in his bed.

His brain just sort of shorted out at that one. Because who in their right fucking mind didn't want Aurora LeMonde? The woman was pure, walking sin. Sex in the body of Aphrodite.

A small knock on the door of their office interrupted their meeting, and not a moment too soon. Dante was about ten seconds away from leaning across the table and smacking the handsome right off Gio's face. Just for being whatever the hell it was that attracted Aurora.

The men turned to see Rose standing shyly in the doorway of the office.

Gio stood up so fast that the papers they'd been studying fluttered to the ground. "Rose!"

Dante raised an eyebrow and watched Gio fumble for the papers and then hurry around the desk to Rose. Was this what he was like with Aurora? Yikes.

"I'll get out of your hair," Dante said. "Nice to see you again, Rose."

"You too," she replied, but she obviously only had eyes for Gio.

Apparently every woman in the world only had eyes for Gio.

Dante left Gio's office and closed the door behind him. He eyed Aurora's closed office door. So that was it. She was in love with someone else.

But then a thought started uncurling in his head. He assumed that she'd been in love with Gio when they'd slept together before, so apparently it wasn't too much of a problem for her. It made his blood pump and his fists clench to think about her longing after Gio, but in a way, it also relieved him.

Finally, Dante had the missing piece of the puzzle. He had all the information. He could finally make a good game plan here. He'd been flying blind before. He considered his options, and as the extremely shrewd businessman he was, a plan started to form.

He knocked once on Aurora's door before he strode into her office, closing the door behind him and sitting down in the chair across from her desk. She sat behind her desk, looking good enough to eat in that clingy silk blouse. She raised her eyebrow at him.

"Can I help you?" Her voice had its usual dose of disdain for him, but there was something else there, too. Nerves.

"Now that you mention it, yes," he said, giving her an exaggerated lascivious grin, hoping to make her smile, and it almost worked.

She bit back her smile and rolled her eyes. "I'm actually glad you're here," she said, leaning back in her chair. "I was wondering if you'd want to collaborate with me on the Sydney expansion project. I can do it on my own, of course, but it's a lot of man-hours, and I was thinking—"

"How long have you been in love with Gio?" He

asked the question casually, his body reclined in his chair like he was a lion eyeing a gazelle from across the prairie.

"I… what?" Her face had gone white, just like it had before when she'd almost fainted last week.

"I just wondered. Has it been weeks? Months? Years? No wonder you slept with me the night of the party. It was the first night he ever brought Rose around." The words were like gravel in his mouth but he spit them out anyway.

She stared at him, her pupils dilated and her breath coming fast. "I…"

"Look, actually, never mind." He held up a hand to stop her. "None of my business. I just figured that you might want someone to talk to about it. It must be hard, being in love with a man who loves someone else."

Her eyes dropped down and for a moment, Dante wanted to drink poison. He was such a fucking dick. But he'd had to land that blow to be able to propose something that would be good for both of them. Mutually beneficial.

She cleared her throat, raising her eyes up again, although they didn't quite meet his. "Do you have a point, Callaghan?"

"Yeah, actually. I think I can help."

She leaned back in her chair, crossing her arms over her chest defensively. "Somehow I find that hard to believe."

He eyed her. "You find it hard to believe that I would want to help you, Aurora? You think so little of me?"

Her expression softened just a little. "No, of course not."

He nodded. "Because what I have to propose would be very beneficial to both of us."

She raised an eyebrow, then gestured for him to go on. "Use me."

She let out a surprised, exasperated laugh. "Excuse me?"

"You need to get over Gio somehow or another, no? You'd rather do it quickly, no? Well, I'm here. I'm obviously willing. Do whatever the hell it is you want to be doing to Gio, but do it to me. Just get it the hell out of your system."

She was looking at him like he'd just spoken in another language. Like the words had to make it through Jello before they got to her. "I'm sorry." She stood, her hands tented on her desk. "I can't possibly be hearing you correctly."

He remained seated. "You heard me just fine. Use my body however you want to use Esposito's and work through some of these feelings. You can't just hold them down forever, Aurora. They've gotta go somewhere. So let them out with me. And then move on."

She closed her eyes and pressed those luscious lips together. "Get the fuck out of my office, Dante."

He rose, knowing when to retreat. "Offer's on the table, LeMonde."

* * *

It was rude. Insulting. Presumptuous. Arrogant. And he

68

was an absolute ASS for proposing it.

Aurora slammed her briefcase closed and slung the strap over her shoulder. She'd never been so incensed in her life. She took a deep, hissing breath and tried to let it out slowly.

This kind of rage couldn't be good for the baby. Between the anger and the constant hum of lust in her belly, this kid was on track to being born an extremely passionate person.

Just like its daddy. Aurora paused at her office door as memories of that night washed over her. He was extremely passionate. She'd never had a more thorough or attentive lover. He'd known what she was feeling before she had. And he'd used every weapon in his arsenal. She shivered.

Her mind shifted from what had been to what could be. Her eyes fell to the chair he'd sat in earlier that day. The way he'd looked, draped across it like a king. God, he was an ass. But he was also very appealing. His hair was longer than it had been that night and she'd found herself wanting to tug on it. Tunnel her hands into it while he buried his mouth between her legs.

Aurora shook her head. She couldn't possibly want that. He was the biggest jerk she'd ever met. He'd actually proposed that she be his fuck toy.

No. Wait. Actually, he was proposing that he would be *her* fuck toy. In a way, it was a little bit sweet.

Aurora shook her head. She must be insane. She blamed it on the pregnancy hormones. Yeah. It was the pregnancy hormones that had her pressing her legs together in her slacks. It was the hormones that had her picturing striding around her desk and straddling him where he sat.

Aurora reached for the door handle of her office but let her hand drop. She really had to get ahold of herself before she went out into the world. She was liable to do something insane if she just walked out there like this. Like confess her love to Gio. Or jump a total stranger.

Aurora looked down at her body. Same old body she'd always had. Tall, curvy, currently filling out a silk shirt and work slacks. No one would guess that there was a river of sexual need pulsing through her right now.

Well, Dante might have guessed it. But she was ignoring that right now.

She took a deep breath. And then another. She was a grown woman in her place of work. She was just going to get in her car and go home and regroup when she got there.

She was going to have to figure out what the hell to do with this considerable need pulsing through her. Sex obviously had to be in her near future in some way, with someone. She couldn't go on much longer feeling like she might pass out if she didn't get off.

Aurora flung the door open to her office and strode to the elevators. Get home. That was the only goal. She jammed the elevator button and froze. Wait, was that…? Oh my god. That was a giggle coming from Gio's office. A woman's giggle.

Aurora whipped her head around to face the other

way. Rose must be in there. In Gio's office right that second. She must be in there, touching him, sitting on his lap, nibbling her way up his neck.

Oh god. Aurora was sick. She was so horny that even the thought of Gio with another woman was turning her on. The elevator doors opened and not a moment too soon. She needed to get the absolute hell away from this office and away from Gio and Rose.

She took the elevator down to the car park and her body trembled. From rage? Yes. From horniness? Yes. From adrenaline and pain? Yes. She felt like she could pull her skin off and dance around. She simultaneously felt as if she could run a marathon and get into bed and sleep for a week.

So far, she was not impressed with pregnancy.

All she knew was that she needed to get a little action. Something to take the edge off. She'd be able to think clearer after that. Aurora pulled out her phone and scrolled to the Tinder app. She'd installed it on a whim a few weeks ago. But she'd yet to open it. Her finger hovered over the little square before she dropped the phone in her lap and leaned forward, forehead against the steering wheel.

God, how pathetic was she? Tindering for a one night stand in the parking structure of her office while Gio was upstairs canoodling with his girlfriend or whatever. Oh yeah, not to mention that she was pregnant and on the search for meaningless sex.

She couldn't have sex with a stranger. What if they

did something weird or awful and it ended up affecting the baby? Aurora would never forgive herself.

Her only options were celibacy or... Dante. Which was insane. Absolutely insane. Why in the name of god in heaven would Aurora ever agree to sleep with the man from whom she was currently trying to conceal a pregnancy.

Although, she didn't exactly LOOK pregnant right now. She would still have some time before she had to come clean with him.

Aurora chewed her lip and picked up her phone. In a way, it would be killing two birds with one stone. She'd get to scratch this god-awful itch with someone who was truly incredible at sex. And she'd inevitably get to know Dante better in the process.

The real question was, did she want to? Did she want to sleep with him again? Aurora's mind took her back to about four a.m. of the night they'd spent together. She'd been straddling his lap as they sat up on his bed, their arms wrapped around one another and his cock buried inside her. He'd had his forehead pressed into her shoulder and her head had fallen back with the pleasure of it all. Something had caught her eye and had her looking to the side. A floor length mirror that hung on the back of his open closet door. It reflected their image back to her.

Aurora had been shocked by what she'd seen. The passion between them had been more than obvious. She'd seen it in every line on her face, the way her fingers dug into him, the straining, trembling grip of her muscles. But even more than that, she'd been shocked by his utter beauty. The fluid, almost violent grace of him as he'd pumped himself into her. His strength, both wildly evident and viciously restrained at the same time. He'd been a fierce, unforgiving lover. But she could see in the mirror exactly how much he was holding back from her, keeping gentle for her. It had been deeply intoxicating to see him coiled and taking and giving.

Aurora's fingers moved over her phone. She was typing and she'd barely even given herself permission to consider the consequences.

Apparently her body had become very bossy since Dante had knocked her up.

Fine. You win. I'm coming over in half an hour.

6

Dante popped the tops off the Indian food that he'd just had delivered, tossed some forks on the counter of the breakfast bar and ripped off some paper towels for napkins. There. That was just fine. If she wasn't happy with that then she could just...

Oh who was he kidding? If she wasn't happy with that, he'd get out his grandmother's china.

Dante scraped a hand over his face and looked down at his work clothes. He usually would have changed out of them by now, but he'd gotten her text right when he'd gotten home and then spent the next half hour frantically getting ready for her. Thank god his Aunt Arlene had been free tonight, otherwise, he might have had to lock Michelle in her room for the next few hours.

Just kidding.

He glanced at the clock. It was almost 45 minutes since she'd texted. Had she changed her mind? He looked at his response to her, texted seconds after she'd texted him.

A single word.

Good.

And then about fifty party hat emojis followed by fifty firework emojis followed by fifty flame emojis.

Maybe not the coolest thing he'd ever done, but he would bet his bank account that it had made her laugh and simultaneously roll her eyes. So it was worth it.

Every muscle in Dante's body froze up tight when he heard a soft knock at his front door.

He strode through the hall, swung open the door and there she was on his front porch. Standing, her hands in the pockets of her slacks, her blonde hair tumbling down her back, and a look on her face he'd seen many, many times before. This was the look she had in a business meeting when she knew she was seconds away from getting what she wanted. If it tented his pants in boardrooms with ten clients sitting next to him, it did it tenfold standing in his front entryway with no one around but the two of them.

"Hi," she said, her voice low and husky.

He immediately stepped back and let her through. He took a few steps toward his kitchen. "I'm glad you came. I took the liberty of ordering some Indian food. If you—"

"Dante."

He turned, looked back over his shoulder and froze. She was toeing out of her shoes and starting to unbutton that clingy silky blouse. The look in her eyes had him forgetting his own name.

"We're not eating. We're not talking." She slid the

shirt from her shoulders and tossed it on the floor. She wore a sheer black bra that was both there and not there. He could see her nipples beading and pressing against the fabric. Next came the button on her slacks. And then she was stepping out of them. Standing there in two scraps of woman magic lingerie that made him want to fall to his knees.

"Were you wearing that at the office today?" His voice was low and gravelly and sounded too intense even to his own ears.

"What?"

"The underwear. That bra. Were you wearing that when you were sitting across from me in your office today."

She nodded.

Dante ripped his work shirt off over his head. Fuck the buttons. He was going for the undershirt as well when she strode toward him.

"Leave it. Undershirts are fucking hot." And then she batted away his hands, undid the button on his pants and then rose up.

They stared at one another for a blinking, breathing second before she lunged forward, planted her mouth at the pulse point on his neck and dragged him to the floor.

Dante thanked god for carpet as they rolled over one another. He lowered his head and suckled her hard through her bra. Aurora cried out and clamped her legs around his waist.

He tried to pin her arms over her head but they

grappled for control. He reached down and clamped her lip between his teeth, still the closest they'd come to kissing, and Aurora moaned, hard. His body went pliant against her and she took advantage of the opportunity.

Using all of her weight and the element of surprise, Aurora rolled them over so that she was on top. There was fire in her eyes as she raised up just enough to fully open his pants, jam them just far enough down his legs to free his cock.

"Jesus. I thought for sure I was embellishing in my memory," she said as she stared at his cock.

He grinned. "Nope."

She looked up at him. Didn't return the smile. "Condom. Now."

He dug into the back pocket of his pants and started to tear it open when she ripped it from his hands, started to do it herself. As she slid the condom down his length, Dante had to grit his teeth and grip the carpet with his hands. It was just too good.

And then she was bracing her hands on his shoulders, raising up over him, poised to take him.

"Aurora, sweetheart, let me—" He reached one hand toward her core, knowing that, small as she was, she was going to have to be extremely ready to be able to take him. He wanted to help her get there. He wanted her to come on his hand, on his mouth. He wanted to make her come a hundred times before he took her. They had all night.

Apparently, she didn't think so, because she slapped his hand away, hooked her panties to the side and sank down on him in one swoop, taking him all the way down to the base.

"Fuck," Dante groaned, his head lifting involuntarily and then rapping back into the floor. Holy god. How the fuck had she been that ready with zero foreplay? But here he was, buried inside her less than thirty seconds after she walked through his door. Dante was not going to waste the opportunity.

His hands found her hips and he gripped her for a second before sliding them up to her gorgeous breasts. He filled his hands with her while Aurora started to ride him. There was no lead up, no finding of her rhythm. She just started riding him hard and kept riding him hard. Her strokes were some addictive cross between vicious and gentle and Dante was losing his mind.

Her eyes were slammed closed, as tight as her fingers, which were digging into his shoulders. Her hair spilled everywhere, tickling his chest, grazing his neck and it gave Dante the insane feeling that she was inching her way inside him as much as he was her.

He planted his feet and started to meet her strokes, taking it to the next level. The slap of skin on skin filled the entryway and Aurora began to moan in earnest now. He could feel her body start to tense and he watched her in amazement. God, she was so responsive. She leaned down even more, ground her clit against him with each stroke. Dante had to look away from the sight of her taking him, lest he blow way too soon.

She was close. So close, he could feel it. He wanted to

take her there. He was just bringing his hand to her clit when she lowered her chest to his, blocking the angle. She ground herself against him in every way, every inch of her body smashing, pinning, possessing him.

He was seeing stars and didn't know how much longer he could possibly hold on through the most exquisite torture of his life. But then she reared up the slightest bit, just enough to plant her plush, soft mouth right on his.

And oh god, he wasn't ready. He had no idea a kiss could be like that. She was swallowing him whole. Every single inch of his body was on fire and her mouth on his was a cool, floral balm. Her warm tongue slipped into his mouth, tentative, sweet, searching. Dante lost his shit.

His arms clamped around her back, cementing her to him as he fucked her hard from the bottom. His mouth opened and his tongue met hers, devouring her. Her flavor exploded through him. The best thing he'd ever tasted in his life. Given he'd tasted her pussy, that was really saying something. He sucked her tongue into his mouth as she moaned, hard and fierce.

Her body clamped down on his over and over again. He swallowed her moans, took them inside of him where they could never escape. Every inch of her was clamping him, down to her hands on the sides of his face. She came so hard and so long that Dante couldn't wait for her to finish. He clenched his eyes closed, his hands made fists on her back, and he poured himself into the condom. For the first time in his life, he cursed the barrier between him and a woman.

* * *

Aurora opened her eyes and slowly realized her hair had completely covered her face. Dante breathed hard underneath her and soon that breath turned into a dark, rumbling chuckle.

"Holy shit. I think you killed me." He reached down behind her bottom to hold the base of the condom as he pulled out of her.

Aurora used the last of her strength to sit up, still straddling him. She tossed her hair back behind her. "I think I killed both of us." She planted a hand on her wildly beating heart and couldn't help but chuckle a little along with him.

"Feeling a little pent up there, gorgeous?" he asked as he climbed to his feet, tied up the condom, and tossed it into the adjacent bathroom trash. Hands on hips, he turned to look at her in all his magnificent glory.

She admired him for a moment before stretching luxuriously. "Just a tad," she said.

She moved to get up, but before she could, he bent down, lifted her up, and carried her into the kitchen where he set her down naked on his granite countertop. The coolness made her hiss, and he smiled. "Now that's a beautiful sight. Hungry after all?"

She swallowed hard, then nodded, grateful he wasn't going to make her talk about what had just happened. They didn't need to talk about all the reasons she'd acted so aggressively just then. All he needed to know was that she'd wanted to have sex, and they had.

Simple as that.

Only as she sat there in her bra and panties, she knew she was kidding herself.

She knew from the moment she'd met him, nothing with Dante had been simple, and that was especially true now.

With apparent reluctance, Dante slowly stepped back, then crossed to the other side of the kitchen and the food he had set out. "I've got Indian for dinner and then some ice cream if you want dessert. I remembered you like Indian food because—" He turned around to face her and completely froze.

"What is it?" she asked when he remained silent.

"Do you have any idea how fucking gorgeous you look. In my kitchen. On my counter. In those two little scraps of lingerie, your hair messy and shiny, your eyes bright and big, and your lips red and smudged and plump."

She blinked, feeling drugged. "Do you have any fucking idea how gorgeous you look? In your kitchen? Almost naked. Your hair messy. Your blue eyes brilliant and dazzling. Your lips red and your body... your body..."

His eyes dead set on her lips, Dante crossed back over the kitchen like a lion stalking prey.

"You let me kiss you just now," he said, his voice almost a whisper.

"Oh. Yeah." Aurora hadn't wanted to kiss him the

night of the party, it had seemed too personal, but tonight she couldn't have stopped herself from kissing him if a tornado had come through the house.

"You're going to let me kiss you again," he said, almost against her lips as he slid between her legs.

"Okay," she whispered, unable to think of anything she wanted more. Okay, she could think of a few things she wanted more, but since she was pretty certain she'd get to have it all, she yearned for his kiss. Right here and now.

And then his lips were on hers. Harsh, demanding, consuming her. There was nothing gentle about the way he was kissing her, crushing her mouth against his, swallowing her alive.

"Dante!" she pulled back from him in surprise when his tongue swept over the front of her teeth.

"Let me," he growled. "Your front teeth drive me insane. So white against your pink little lips and just a little crooked."

"Hey!" she pulled back again, not sure whether to be offended or flattered. She planted a hand over her mouth. "I hate my crooked front teeth."

"Don't," he demanded, tugging her hand down. "They're so fucking hot."

She looked at him like he was insane. "Crooked teeth are hot?"

"Yours are," he insisted, leaning forward and sucking her bottom lip into his mouth for a second. "Something about the little imperfection. I don't know. It just drives me wild. It's like you're this complete and utter goddess.

Aphrodite. Cleopatra. And then you have this little perfectly imperfect thing that reminds me that you're human." He traced one hand roughly up her side, cupped her breast in a possessive way. "It reminds me that you're touchable." He stepped even closer to her, pressing her heat into his stomach and tangling his tongue with hers for just a second. "Fuckable."

"Oh." The word was breathless, desperate as she gasped and clasped her feet around his waist. They'd just fucked not ten minutes ago, there was no way he was going there again, right? The man was almost forty. But, whoops, yeah, that thing she was feeling against her core was definitely not his leg. Wow. The man had stamina.

She tore her mouth away from his and took a gasping breath, resting her forehead against his shoulder for just a second. There were feelings bubbling up inside her that were making this moment very confusing. She was exhausted yet wired, sated yet hungry, wary and giddy all at once. She knew the smart thing would be to retreat, regroup, take a beat to organize her thoughts in the privacy of her own home.

But all of those thoughts completely fled as Dante began to kiss his way down her neck. And over her breasts. He paid lavish, selfish attention to her breasts as he unclipped her bra, then laving each of her breasts with his tongue and teeth, using his stubble to make her nipples stand tall and beg for him.

She leaned back on her hands on the counter as he continued to kiss down her stomach, nuzzling her navel and then finally, finally, letting his mouth close over her core. She still wore her underwear, so she couldn't feel him in great detail, but his hot, wicked mouth already had her clenching and raising up off the counter.

That night they'd spent together, he'd tasted her off of his fingers, off of her own fingers, but he hadn't directly gone down on her. And the thought that he might be about to do just that had Aurora's breath coming in pants.

He knelt before her and stripped her panties away, then took one more second to strip his undershirt away. He tossed the discarded clothes onto the floor beside him. For some reason, the sight of her slinky black underwear mixed and tossed with his utilitarian undershirt was wildly erotic to her. Aurora found herself spreading her legs for him with no prompting necessary.

"Good girl," he growled, looking up from between her legs. He held her eyes as he leaned forward and planted his mouth over her.

Aurora's body went fully electric. She wouldn't have been surprised if blue light was shooting out of her fingertips, out the top of her head. She'd never felt anything like this before. This man was deeply skilled, that much was for sure, but she'd also never been in the path of this much passion before.

His hands were planted on either of her thighs, holding her fully open for him. He kissed her as if she were the love of his life, like they'd been separated by war for decades. He kissed her pussy like he was suffocating and she was air.

And then his tongue was plunging into her and the making love part was over. Now he was just downright fucking her pussy with his mouth. He plunged into her over and over, dexterously touching every part of her. When he slid his mouth upward and sucked her clit, tonguing and sucking and groaning, Aurora plunged over the cliff and to the other side of pleasure. Her body quaked and shook and liquefied for him. He suckled her through her orgasm and then stood up, immediately cushioning her head against his shoulder as she went weak around him.

She was vaguely aware of the sound of a condom wrapper tearing. He threaded his fingers through her hair and tipped her head back. She was shocked at what she saw on his face. A terrible need for her, etched into every line. He was no longer the smooth-talking Dante she saw in boardrooms or the flirty, sexy Dante who sidled up to her at social engagements. This was full-on pirate Dante, soldier Dante, sex Dante. He was tense and coiled and on edge.

The hand in her hair tightened, just to the edge of pain, before he slid it around to her chin. He held her face in place as the head of his cock nudged her entrance, pushing in just a scant inch.

"You going to let me take it again, baby?" he asked her, and his words had her pussy clamping again, her heart racing.

"Yes. God, yes."

He plunged into her completely, and both of them groaned. His strokes were short and fierce and measured as if he were digging inside her for some special secret. And god did he find it. The angle had him pressing against something that Aurora had never felt before. It felt like an orgasm that started from deep inside her, but she hadn't even known that was possible. She tensed her legs around his waist and let him take her there. Let him show her all of it.

She clung and exploded into a kaleidoscope of stars as she screamed into his mouth. She felt him tense and let go as well, and all she could do was hold him tighter.

7

"Food," Aurora groaned into his neck where she'd buried her face. The aftershocks had gone, and all that was left was a full-bodied exhaustion. An absolute need for nourishment like she'd never known before. "Now."

Dante chuckled and disentangled them, wincing as he pulled out of her. She immediately missed the heat of his skin against hers, but something kept her from pulling him toward her again.

He held out a hand to help her hop down from the counter.

"This food's going to need some reheating. If you want you can wash up in my bathroom while I get the food ready. You remember where it is?"

He jerked his chin toward the stairs and the room that Aurora remembered very well.

Aurora nodded and shivered. She hadn't realized the air had been so chilly in here until she was standing there completely naked, covered in a thin layer of sweat. "How'd you know I'd want a bath?"

He shrugged. "You're practically swaying on your feet right now. Go relax upstairs and I'll let you know when dinner is ready."

Aurora frowned, but she turned and walked up the stairs. This was really not how she'd thought this was going to go. She really thought she was going to get here, bang him, and leave. But he'd ordered them dinner? What the heck was his angle here? There was no way she was leaving without eating some of that food but he wasn't wrong that she was basically dead on her feet. A bath would actually be really nice right about now.

She ignored his bedroom and the onslaught of memories it brought back and walked straight into his adjoining bathroom. She sighed. A claw foot tub. Perfect.

She ran the water into it, but couldn't find any bubbles to add. She couldn't help rolling her eyes at the well-stocked drawer of condoms he had. Fat lot of good that had done them.

Normally, she liked a piping hot bath. However, her OBGYN had warned her against that in her first trimester, so Aurora settled for a mildly warm one. Still, she had no complaints when she piled her hair in a messy bun and slipped into the warm water. Heaven.

She made quick work with the bar of soap on the ledge, reveling in the manly smell of it.

All clean, her eyes fluttered closed and she hovered somewhere between thoughts and dreams and memories, each muscle in her body slowly relaxing.

"Sweetheart."

His voice had her eyes flinging open, but she didn't tense back up. He stood in the doorway of the bathroom, barefoot and shirtless, his work slacks slung low over his hips. He crossed his arms over his chest and gave her a pained expression.

"You trying to invite me in?" He nodded toward her legs, one of which was drawn up, her foot planted on the edge of the tub. It had been a natural pose for Aurora to strike in the tub, but she could see now that it was alluring. She was opening herself for him.

The thought struck her like lightning. She pictured him crawling into the tub, slacks and all, the water spilling over the sides. Her core clenched around nothing, needing to be filled again. But a different hunger won out.

"Food," she croaked again.

Dante threw his head back and laughed. "Fair enough, gorgeous. It's all ready downstairs. I brought your clothes up." He nodded toward a pile of folded clothes he'd set on the counter. "But you can find something in the closet if you want to get more comfortable."

And then he was gone. Leaving her be. Aurora had been certain from the minute she'd seen him in the doorway that he was going to stay and watch her get out of the tub. But no, he gave her space. And had folded her clothes.

She wrinkled her nose at the new information. Weird. It somehow didn't fit the playboy image she had of him in her head. Well, part of the reason she was here was to learn more about him, so she supposed it was important to approach things with an open mind.

She dried off and despite being terribly tempted to go through his clothes and pick out something to wear, slipped back into her clothes. She had to maintain some distance, after all.

She peeked at herself in the mirror and was surprised at what she saw. Besides the professional clothing, she looked like she could be a college girl hanging out at home after class. Her hair was piled up on top of her head, her makeup washed off from the bath. Her skin was flushed and slightly pink. And her eyes were… blurry? Relaxed? Happy?

Strange. Feeling vaguely suspicious of what her own reflection was telling her, Aurora headed downstairs. She was fairly certain she could eat an entire buffet right now. All-you-can-eat would lose money tonight.

She had laser vision as she bounced down the stairs and perched herself on the bar stool at the breakfast bar. Dante, bless him, had already loaded her plate with food and was just setting out a glass of ice water for her.

"I also have beer? Wine? A stiff whiskey to put the color back in your cheeks?" He surveyed her, cocking his head to one side. "Actually, strike that. The bath did that just fine."

She met his gaze for a moment, and something electric passed between them before she deliberately tucked into her food. She waved her hand to show him that water was fine.

He leaned over the bar and watched her eat with a vaguely amazed look in his eye. "You look about 18 with your hair piled up like that and no makeup."

She finally looked back up at him, swallowing what was in her mouth and taking a big gulp of water. "You wanna see some ID?"

He laughed. "I'll take your word for it."

* * *

Dante slid onto the stool across from her and started eating. He couldn't get a read on her. She seemed relaxed and sated and obviously very hungry. But he couldn't tell what the hell else she was feeling.

He wasn't sure why it was so important. Regardless of what she was feeling, they'd still done something amazing together. He thought of the look in her eyes when she'd come through the door. The way she'd looked when she'd taken him inside her. Yeah. He was pretty much on cloud nine right now. It was ridiculous, but he felt like his bar stool was a helium balloon, floating him up into the stratosphere.

Some of her ravenous hunger taken care of, Aurora took a deep breath and started eating at a more human pace. As she did so, her gaze scanned his home.

He wondered if she was surprised by what she saw.

"You know, your house is cuter than I thought it would be. It's actually like a house."

He raised an eyebrow and bit into a samosa. "What were you picturing?"

"I dunno. Lots of chrome and glass. Some condo high above the city where you could look down on everybody. A room designated for your sex swings."

Dante threw his head back and laughed. Really laughed. "Well, you pretty much described my old condo down to a T. Except for the sex swing part. But yeah, I sold that and moved here when I got custody of my sister. She needed something a little warmer. More homey."

* * *

Aurora dropped her eyes from him and stared at the food on her plate, hardly seeing it. He'd surprised her again. As if his house hadn't already done that enough.

It was homey. Colored jars of herbs and spices on the counter, an ugly little handmade something hanging in the window above the sink, mismatched placemats on the big dinner table behind her. And pictures on the walls. Lots of them. Artsy ones and family ones. What the hell?

And what the fuck did he mean 'custody'. He was raising his little sister? Dante Callaghan was living in a house in suburbia raising a kid? Why the hell hadn't she known this? She'd known the man for four fucking years.

He narrowed his eyes in confusion as he studied her reaction. "You didn't know? About my sister?"

Aurora cleared her throat and took a grateful sip of her ice water. "I knew that you two were close. I met her at that company picnic a few years ago. Remember?"

"I remember." His eyes were dark and inscrutable.

"But I didn't know you had custody of her. I assumed you brought her in order to…"

Aurora trailed off, appalled at the ugliness of her assumption and appalled that she'd been about to say it out loud.

But Dante merely quirked a smile, dug out more channa masala from a carton to put on his plate. "You assumed I brought her as some sort of pick-up tactic for the women at the picnic? A way to soften up the ladies so I could get a little taste of tail?"

Aurora shrugged, her cheeks flaming with her deep embarrassment. "I guess."

Dante took it in good humor, chuckling and sighing. "Well, I gotta say, I didn't expect it—how hot some women found it when I told them I was raising a kid alone."

Aurora laughed, pushing her food around on her plate. She was still reeling. Both from the discovery that Dante was raising his sister and from the fact that she barely knew him at all.

"I'm sorry, I don't mean to assume the worst about you."

He shrugged. If she'd hurt his feelings, he hid it well. "I think my reputation often precedes me. Whether it's an earned reputation or not."

What did that mean? That he wasn't a total player? Aurora's head spun. This was a lot of new information all at once. She had about a hundred questions but she found herself snapping her mouth shut. She'd already insulted him enough and was too nervous to say anything else.

Dante scooped more food onto her empty plate, eyeing her. "It's okay, Aurora. You can ask questions. You want to know more about my situation with Michelle?"

She looked up. It seemed rude to pry, but he was offering and more information was a huge part of the reason she was here in the first place. "Your parents are…"

"Both alive. My mother is flighty, unreliable, rich as chocolate and somewhere in Thailand right now. And she's not Michelle's mother. We're related through our dad. Who is…" He paused, a dark expression coming over his face. "Unfit to be a father. So, when Michelle's mother passed away when she was five, I knew that it was up to me to make sure she had a good life. It took about a year, but I gained custody over her when she was six."

"How old is she now?" Aurora asked, looking around the house for more clues that a little girl lived there. She saw a purple article of clothing tossed over a chair in the corner of the living room.

"Ten going on thirty. I swear, she's smarter than I am."

Aurora soaked in the little smile on his face as he talked about his sister and felt, for a moment, like she was staring into the sun. She felt like there were two Dante Callaghans. The one who had hit on her relentlessly for years and the one who lovingly grinned into his food when he was talking about the little sister he was raising. A headache started to form behind her left eye.

"So how come you never bring her around? You've had her for four years and the only time I've ever met her was two years ago at that picnic?"

"She hates doing work related stuff. Every once in a while I'll bring her into my office and she'll entertain herself for an hour. And after that I pretty much wish I'd never been born." He grinned again.

Aurora felt as if her stomach had turned into a fist. A giant, clenching fist.

"But the picnic was outdoors and there were going to be other kids there, so she wanted to go. Plus," he raked a hand over his stubble for a second, a look coming into his eyes that she'd never seen before. "I was what you'd call a nervous new parent. I was so scared when I first took her in. We barely knew each other, and her mom had just died. I just wanted her to be comfortable and happy. So we spent a lot of time one-on-one. And I guess I just got used to it that way."

Aurora filed the information away for later. She felt like she could barely breathe, let alone comprehend what he was saying right now. She thought back to the little girl from the office picnic. Rat's nest hair, a Little League softball t-shirt. She'd been sweet. She'd asked Aurora to take her to the restroom because Dante wasn't allowed in. Another memory trickled through. "She got hurt at that picnic. Banged her knee or something?"

Dante's eyes darkened again. "We left early for the

hospital."

"The hospital for a banged knee?"

Dante pushed his empty plate away from him and reached for his water. "She has a blood disorder called Von Willebrand's. It's similar to hemophilia, for all intents and purposes. And any time she gets a bruise, she risks internal hemorrhaging."

"Wow. Oh my god, Dante. I'm so sorry."

"It's manageable with regular health care, but we have to take stuff like that really seriously."

"Wow," she repeated again. Aurora lowered her chin to her hand, pressing her eyes closed against the pain that was growing in her head. This was all so much. Almost too much. Definitely too much.

"You alright?" He reached across the breakfast bar and cupped her elbow, a look of concern etched onto his face.

"Yes." She waved a hand through the air and pushed her empty plate away from her the same as he had. "I guess I'm just having trouble reconciling Dante Callaghan, Moneybags Ladies Man, with Dante Callaghan, Devoted Brother."

Dante leaned back in his chair, a serious look on his face. "There's only one Dante Callaghan, Aurora."

"Sure, sure." She stood and started clearing plates. "I guess I'm just surprised at how little we know one another."

"Yeah, well, blame yourself for that one," he said as he came up behind her while she started loading up the dishwasher. He nuzzled his nose into the crook of her neck. "You're the one who's been keeping me at arm's length for years. Hmmm. You smell like my soap."

Aurora turned in his arms, squinted at him, and tried to get her brain to catch up with reality. "Dante Callaghan, family man."

He scoffed and tightened his arms around her waist. "Family man might be pushing it a little far. Michelle and I have made it work for us over the years, but I'm not exactly a 'kids' person." He shuddered. "Raising her has been hard enough and she's like the best kid ever. I'm not interested in doing it again."

Well.

Well.

That answered that.

Aurora gulped. Okay. That was information. He hadn't said it to hurt her. She couldn't allow herself to linger over the pain and fear settling into her stomach.

It was simply a fact about him. He didn't want kids. She wasn't getting closer to him because he wanted to be World's Best Dad to the kid in her belly. No. She was getting closer to him in order to figure out who the hell he actually was. And she'd just gotten a shit ton of information all at once.

Any of the fatigue that dinner and a bath had soothed instantly came back full force. The pain behind her eye increased ten fold and the only thing Aurora wanted to do was crawl under her covers and sleep for a week. His arms around her waist suddenly felt as if they were trapping her.

She stepped out of his grasp and smoothed her shirt down with one hand. "I'm going to go."

She inwardly winced at the rude note in her tone, but she couldn't really help it. She needed to get the hell out of here.

"Oh," he cleared his throat. "Sure."

"Thanks for dinner," she said over her shoulder as she padded down the hall toward her shoes.

"Anytime." There was something in his voice that wasn't usually there, but Aurora was currently full up on things to interpret. He followed her to the door and opened it for her, reaching out and clasping her elbow as she passed.

Was he looking for a kiss?

"What are the odds that this happens again, Aurora?"

She shrugged, completely unable to answer that question. "I'll let you know." And then, before he could kiss her, before she could kiss him the way she was seriously wanting to, she walked out the door and forced herself not to look back.

* * *

Dante watched her go. He watched her get into the driver's seat and pull smoothly down his driveway. He watched her taillights disappear. He held onto the doorknob as if it were the only thing holding him to earth. He couldn't believe that that had just happened. He turned and looked back in his entryway. Well, they'd certainly christened it.

That helium balloon that had been growing underneath him suddenly popped with a vicious, stomach sinking finality. The reason they'd christened his entryway settled over him.

She'd come over to do what he'd propositioned. She'd come over to use him. To exorcise her feelings for Gio.

Had she thought of Gio while they'd been together? Had she left because she'd decided Dante had been a piss poor substitute for the man she really wanted?

Dante frowned and closed the front door behind him. He couldn't fault her for doing exactly what he'd told her to do. But as he stepped back into the kitchen to box up the rest of the food, he couldn't ignore the clenching in his gut.

She'd been fucking him, kissing him, sure. But she probably had been thinking of Gio.

And that was something that angered and saddened him in ways he couldn't comprehend.

His plan had backfired and he had no one to blame but himself.

8

Aurora frowned at the single red tulip currently sitting in a simple glass vase in the cup holder of her car.

She had no idea what possessed her to bring that particular flower home. Dante had sent her an entire flower shop since that first night she'd slept with him all those weeks ago. Armfuls of flowers everyday. And then, this morning, she'd come into work and there it had been. A single, juicy little tulip in a simple glass vase.

And her dang heart had skipped.

It had taken her a few days to sort through all of her feelings and she still wasn't there. She wasn't sure she'd ever be.

She pulled into the driveway of her mother's small bungalow and, on a whim, brought the tulip with her into the house.

"Bonjou, Manman," Aurora greeted her mother in Creole. Hello, Mama.

"Bonjou, piti. My lamou." Hello, daughter. My love.

Cedalie paused in the solitaire she was playing for a kiss on the cheek from her girl. "I can see by the look on that face of yours that the flower is not for me."

"What? Oh." Aurora looked down at the tulip she had firmly in her hand, genuinely confused as to why she'd brought it inside. Not like anything would have happened to it in the car. "No, it was a gift to me. But I'll leave it for you, Mama."

Cedalie clucked her tongue. "No, piti, it's bad energy to give away a gift as personal as that one. You know that."

"Sure," Aurora said absently, sitting next to her mother at the small kitchen table and fiddling absently with two small rose quartz crystals that sat next to the deck of cards. Aurora's fingers tensed over the stones as she sensed a funny vibration from them, subtle, but recognizable.

Cedalie lightly slapped Aurora's hand away. "Don't touch. Those haven't been cleansed yet."

Cedalie was talking about the energy of the crystals being cleansed, which her mother would do by burning sage. Aurora pulled her hands back. She wasn't as talented as her mother was, but Aurora wasn't immune to the knowledge.

Cedalie sat back, shuffling the cards in her skilled hands. As she did so, she stared at Aurora, likely studying her aura as she was prone to do.

"Put that tea in a jar," Cedalie said, nodding toward the counter where a pot of tea was steeping. "We'll take it on our walk."

"I'm not in the mood for a walk, Mama. I'm tired."

"You need a walk, trust your mother."

Aurora didn't argue further. She poured the earthy smelling tea into a little glass jar and waited by the door for her mother to slip on her tennis shoes. Cedalie tucked her hand through Aurora's arm and they started their stroll through Cedalie's neighborhood.

The neighborhood was filled with families just trying to get by. The homes were often shabby, but clean. Owned, not rented. Neighbors sat on their porches with a drink or a cigarette, some of them picking away at instruments.

Cedalie waved at a few people as they walked. Aurora couldn't help the surge of affection for her mother. Her black hair shot through with silver, the small green crystal on a chain around her neck, the plain blue hoodie accented with the colorful scarf. God. How would she ever get through this if not for Cedalie?

"I'm confused, Mama."

"I can see that, bebe."

"In my aura?"

Cedalie nodded.

"He doesn't want children." Aurora watched the sun set in the distance and almost immediately felt calmer for having said her truth. The truth that had been choking her since her evening with Dante a few days ago.

"No one knows what they want, Aurora. Like I said, time tells the truth."

Aurora said nothing. Just took a sip of the tea out of the jar, grimaced at the flavor, and nodded her head.

"You keep doing what you're doing, daughter. You're doing right by your child, getting to know what blood your child will carry. You get to know the father, it will only serve you. The difference between walking into a room with your eyes open or closed."

Aurora nodded again. "So you think I should keep doing what I've been doing?"

"The baby is calm. You're doing right. You're doing right."

Twenty minutes later, Aurora sat in her car and contemplated what her mother said. Then she finally did what she'd been wanting to do ever since she left Dante's house. She texted him.

Chances of us happening again = 100%. Tomorrow night?

* * *

The night after Aurora texted him, she showed up at his house after work. This time, they'd managed to make it to his bedroom, but not by much. And then a few more tomorrows after that came and went in the same way. She'd come over, they'd fuck one another's brains out, and then he'd feed her. It never failed to amuse him how ravenous she was after sex.

Soon, two weeks had gone by and Dante was under the distinct impression that he was starting to date Aurora

LeMonde. He just wasn't sure that she'd agree.

He stared out the window of his office, twenty stories up in downtown Los Angeles, and tapped a pencil against his desk.

He couldn't remember a time in his life when he'd been so satisfied and so frustrated at the same time. He had her. He had her many times a week. That body, those lips, that voice, that hair. It was his. Ripe for the taking.

And at the same time, he didn't have her.

She was in love with Gio. And if she wasn't thinking of Gio during sex, then she certainly was knocking on Dante's door to work off some energy after a day of working side by side with Gio.

The pencil snapped in his fingers.

He knew he had an ego. What man didn't? But it was more than that. He didn't want Aurora just because she was another man's and it pricked at him. He wanted her because he wanted her. And yes, because *she* wanted him. Plain and simple.

"What's wrong with you?" Michelle asked from the other side of his desk, her head popping up from the pages of a Percy Jackson novel. Her after school program had been cancelled today so Dante had had to pick her up and bring her to work while he finished up a few things.

She didn't usually mind an hour of killing time, but he knew they were fast approaching the danger zone. The time of night when she'd be hungry, tired, and bored.

"Nothing." He tossed the two halves of the broken pencil into the trash and kicked out from behind his desk.

"You ready to get going, kid?"

She nodded her messy brown hair. "Finally. I was about to gnaw off my own arm."

"From hunger or boredom?" He picked up Michelle's black and white striped backpack and threw it over his shoulder, leaning down and helping her stand up.

"Hunger, obvi. I haven't had anything since lunch."

"Well, why didn't you say anything, pipsqueak?" He looked back at her and opened his office door. "I woulda gotten you something from the vending machine. I'm not a monster."

"Oh."

Dante whipped around to face the open door of his office. Aurora was standing there, her bag slung across her shoulders and a file in her hands. She wore a coral colored dress, tight at the waist, with a pattern of little cut outs around the neck that gave tantalizing glimpses of her golden skin underneath. Her hair was swept halfway back in a knot and the rest fell around her shoulders.

Dante clapped his mouth closed before he drooled all over himself. "Aurora."

"I'm sorry," she said, taking half a step back. Her eyes zipped from the backpack on Dante's back to Michelle's messy hair and the oversized t-shirt that currently had a jelly stain on the front. "I didn't mean to interrupt. I just wanted to drop off the Peterson contract. I saw the light on from downstairs and thought…"

Was she rambling? Was she blushing? Peterson contract, his ass. Dante would bet any amount of money that she'd come to fuck. Well. He would not have complained.

Alas, hungry kid, school night, his life. "No need to apologize. We were just headed out. You remember my kid sister, Michelle?" He pulled Michelle in front of him and gave her shoulder a little squeeze to remind her what to do next.

"Hi," Michelle said, holding out her hand for a shake. "You're Aurora, right? You took me to the bathroom at that picnic thing a few years ago."

Aurora bent to shake hands with the girl, her hair falling over her shoulder. "Good memory."

"Dante was just going to take me to get some Chinese food. Wanna come with us?"

Dante dropped his eyes down to Michelle as she tipped her head back and grinned up at him. "I was?" he asked wryly.

"Sure," she shrugged. "Least you can do after starving me up in this cage all afternoon."

"Yeah. Callaghan Inc. is a real Alcatraz," he said, gently shoving her forward and flicking the light off in his office as the three of them walked toward the elevator.

Aurora was still peeking around at both of them, presumably having a bit of trouble believing what her eyes were seeing.

"What do you say, gorgeous? Wanna join us for dinner?"

"Um. Sure," she said, laying one hand over her belly in a way that made Dante think she must be really hungry.

"Can we do it take out, Coco?" Michelle asked, naturally taking his hand as they exited the elevator toward the parking lot.

"Coco?" Aurora repeated in complete disbelief, humor and surprise warring in her eyes.

"An old nickname from when she was younger," Dante muttered, ruffling Michelle's hair. He could have gone a long time without Aurora LeMonde knowing that his little sister sometimes called him Coco. "Why do you want to do it take out, Michelle?"

She opened the backseat of the car and started climbing in. "One, because then we can eat at home which is better because the air conditioning in that restaurant is flipping cold. And two, because they only give you the good fortune cookies if you order take out. You get the boring ones if you eat in."

"She's right," Dante said, smiling at Aurora, who was still looking a little shell-hocked. "The take out is all around better."

"Oh. Okay." Aurora brushed a hand over her hair. "Well, maybe I'll just go home then."

"No! Come have dinner with us, Aurora! Dante never brings friends home. Please?"

* * *

Aurora hesitated, but how could she say no to the little girl with the messy hair, big blue eyes and the big, hopeful smile? And how could she say no to the man whose shoulders stretched that business suit like it was their job? The man who still had his little sister's backpack over his shoulder. The man whose big hopeful smile matched, exactly, the little girl's beside him.

"Okay," she heard herself saying. "I'll follow you. Will you order me—"

"Orange chicken, one egg roll, one spring roll, and cold sesame noodles? Yeah. I remember from last time," Dante said with a wink.

"Okay," she said again in that same small voice. Her brain was going a mile a minute here. What the hell was even going on?

Aurora walked to her car, determined not to look back, but of course, she did. She did it just in time to see Dante toss Michelle's backpack in the back seat and say something in a low, firm voice. Michelle lifted her hands in innocence and said something back that had Dante chuckling and shaking his head.

Aurora slid into the front seat of her car. Knowing he took care of a kid and watching it happen were two very different things, she realized. Over the last few weeks, she'd finally started to wrap her head around the new Dante. The one who basically had a kid. She'd gone over there enough times, seen Michelle's stuff strewn around, listened to him mention her here and there.

Aurora had thought she had a handle on the whole thing. But apparently not. Seeing them together, their obvious rapport, their ease with one another, had really thrown her for a loop.

Dante never brings friends home.

Michelle's words echoed through Aurora's head as she followed their car through downtown Los Angeles, to the Chinese food place and then back to Dante's house. Did that mean that he never brought women home? Or at least never let them meet Michelle?

Then why the hell was he inviting her to dinner? He could have introduced her as a work colleague, taken the damn contract and told her he'd see her on Monday. He didn't have to invite her into family time.

Aurora forced her hands to loosen on the steering wheel. She took a deep, cleansing breath and rolled down the window for some fresh air as she rolled up the driveway.

She'd had another doctor's appointment that morning and the doctor had warned her, again, about the negative effects of stress. She insisted that Aurora find some outlets to bring more calm into her life.

So, either Aurora could fret and piece apart every second of what was about to go down. Or she could relax, eat some orange chicken and hang out with someone who seemed like a very good kid.

She supposed she was going to have to get used to hanging out with a kid. Aurora cleared her throat. She was going to have to get used to it alright, just not with Dante around. After all, Dante had already admitted he didn't want kids, and she wasn't about to make him feel obligated to take care of her.

Aurora sighed deeply and stepped out of the car,

careful not to slam the door. She had arrived a few minutes later than they had and she found herself knocking on the front door as Michelle pulled it open, a huge grin on the little girl's face and an even bigger book in one hand.

"You want to look at my new book while Coco sets out dinner?" Michelle asked holding up the huge tome and stepping backwards so that Aurora could come inside.

"Sure," Aurora said as she stepped in and kicked off her shoes. "What's the story about?"

"It's not really a story, it's more of an encyclopedia, I guess," Michelle said. "Dante got it for me for my birthday but he says it's too boring to read with me."

Aurora laughed. "Is that so?"

"Yeah," Michelle said, climbing up onto the big plush couch in their living room and shoving aside some pillows to make room for Aurora. "But he thinks everything Harry Potter is boring."

"Excuse me?" Aurora stopped in her tracks and put one hand over her heart. "You've gotta be kidding me. He doesn't like Harry Potter? I didn't realize the man was a lunatic."

Michelle laughed and flipped the book open. "Totally."

* * *

When Dante found Aurora and Michelle, he wasn't prepared for how affected he'd feel at the sight of his two favorite females together. Aurora had her feet demurely tucked under her, the coral dress straining around her hips and breasts as she leaned over Michelle's shoulders to get a better look at the pages.

"There it is!" Aurora said pointing at the page. "I knew it was a total tongue twister. *Peskipiksi Pesternomi.*"

"Pepsi pipsi Pepperoni," Michelle tried to repeat it and had both of them dissolving into laughter.

"Sounds like something on the menu at a pizzeria."

The girls swiveled their heads around to look at him and Dante was much obliged to see Aurora's eyes give him a quick scan up and down. He was pretty certain her eyes lingered a bit longer on the dishtowel at his shoulder, but he couldn't be certain.

"Your sister tells me that you're not a Harry Potter fan." Aurora lifted an eyebrow at him.

"Oh god." Dante sagged against the door jamb. "Not you too. I'm surrounded by nerds."

"Nerdy is the new cool, Coco," Michelle said, getting up from the couch and strolling toward the kitchen.

He took the dishtowel off his shoulder and whipped it up tight, snapping it out in the air a scant inch from Michelle's waggling behind. Michelle merely cackled with laughter and took off for the kitchen.

Dante took in Aurora's expression. "You know I'd never actually snap her with this, right?"

"Of course, because of the Von Willebrand's?"

"You remembered the name of it."

"Remember it? I Googled the crap out of it when I got home."

The fact that she'd cared enough to Google Michelle's condition meant the world to him. In that moment, he wanted to sweep her into his arms and kiss her, but instead he let her walk past him toward the kitchen. She didn't get to see the way he watched her walk away, for once not focusing on the sway of her hips but rather, just the air around her, just the way she moved through his house, toward his little sister who waited, her feet swinging on the stool in the kitchen. She didn't turn, so she didn't get to see it.

But it was there. And it was real. And he felt it.

* * *

After dinner, Michelle wanted to watch a movie and Aurora found herself in the peculiar position of saying yes to the invitation without a single reservation. Dinner had been fun, full of teasing and laughter and so much food all of them groaned and held their bellies and begged for mercy.

And now Aurora sat next to Michelle on the floor, combing through the endless DVD collection that Dante kept hidden in a chest underneath the flat screen.

"Oh, let's have mercy on him," Aurora whispered to Michelle when the little girl pulled out her collection of Harry Potter movies. "What about this one?"

She held out Inside Out.

"Sure!" Michelle said, reaching for it. As she did, a necklace fell forward from the neck of her loose t-shirt.

"That's pretty," Aurora said, reaching for the chain of the necklace and deftly avoiding the clear crystal that hung on the end.

"Aunt Arlene gave it to me last year, she said it's a magic stone."

"Clear quartz isn't magical, really."

Michelle's eyes dimmed but Aurora kept going. "But it is very powerful."

Michelle's eyes lit right up again. "Really?"

"Oh, yeah. It's a healing crystal. But yours won't work right now."

"Why not?"

"Well," Aurora rose, held out her hand to Michelle to help the little girl up. "Crystals have energy fields. And so do you. And crystals can kind of be used like energy soap, to clean up your energy field."

"Cool." Michelle's eyes were huge and riveted on Aurora. When Aurora glanced his way, she could see that Dante's eyes were riveted on her as well. She swallowed hard, naturally resistant to sharing this part of herself that she normally kept close to her heart, but she'd already piqued Michelle's interest. Plus she wanted Michelle to get the healing qualities of the crystal, so…

"If you use one crystal to clean too many things, or if you wear it for a long time without cleaning it, it gets kind of dirty itself," she explained.

"Like if you use a rag to dust too many shelves, the rag gets all dirty."

"Exactly." Aurora brushed the little girl's messy hair

back from her face in an absent gesture. "So right now your crystal has all sorts of energetic grit and grime. We have to cleanse it if you wanna keep wearing it."

"How?"

"Well, my mother uses sage smoke, but I don't suppose you have any of that." Aurora raised an eyebrow at Dante and he raised one right back. "Well, in a pinch there are a few other things you can do. Clear, fresh, running water is one or dirt where something new is growing. Like a garden."

"We don't have one."

"Alright, then the last resort is moonlight."

"Really?" Michelle was vibrating on her feet.

"Sure. You find a patch of moonlight and lay it there all night, and in the morning it will be safe to wear again."

Michelle was off like a shot, unclasping her necklace and flipping off the lights so that she could locate the best patch of moonlight.

"Where'd you learn all that?" Dante asked gently before tugging Aurora onto the couch next to him.

She shrugged. "My mother is Louisiana Creole. Born in the bayou and then lived in New Orleans most of her life. She has a different set of beliefs and understandings than you Northerners do. But it's not that uncommon down there."

"If I don't believe a word of it is she going to take a lock of my hair, sew it to a doll and prick it with a pin?"

Aurora frowned at him. "She's not Voodoo. Or Hoodoo."

"What the hell is Hoodoo?"

Aurora threw her hands in the air. "Google it for fuck sakes. I'm just saying that my mother is not crazy. And neither am I."

Dante stilled for a second. Well, most of him stilled. His hand, however, kept tracing patterns on the silky skin of her thigh. "So you believe it too. That wasn't just for Michelle's benefit."

Aurora sighed. Sometimes she missed New Orleans so much she could barely breathe. This would never be something she'd have to explain on a date down there. "It's easy to believe in something that is real for you."

He pulled back from her. "What do you mean 'real'?"

Aurora dragged a hand down her face. "I don't usually talk about this stuff to people who I want to see me as a competent business woman."

"Aurora, I stopped thinking of you as just a competent business woman the night I fucked you against the steering wheel of my car."

"Shhh."

"If you're asking whether or not I'm going to stop thinking you're competent because you believe in mystical juju whatever, well, no. I won't stop thinking you're competent. As far as I'm concerned, you're the engine behind that company."

Her eyes narrowed on his, thoughtful. He really thought that she was that essential to Gio's company?

"Alright, then," Aurora said. "If you're so eager to know, I just mean that I know energy like that is real because I can feel it, sense it. Auras are real because I can see them, sense them. You call it 'belief', but I call it 'reality'."

Dante narrowed his eyes just as Michelle's bare feet slapped back into the room. "I did it. There was a big patch in the laundry room. How will I know if it's clean in the morning?"

"In the morning, soak it in some salt water for at least a few hours. Just to be safe."

Michelle nodded. And then with the guilelessness of a child, climbed onto the couch between Dante and Aurora.

"Brought it," she said to Dante, holding up a small nose spray of some kind. "It's time for my medicine," she said to Aurora.

Aurora had read about that. Children were able to take some of their Von Willebrand's medicine as nose spray. It saved them from having to get shots every other day, which for a blood clotting disorder, was important.

Dante helped administer the nose spray, set it aside, and then gathered Michelle next to him. His arm snaked along the back of the couch and played with the ends of Aurora's hair.

The movie blinked on. As she watched the colorful film, felt the warmth of the little girl's shoulder pressing into hers, felt Dante playing with her hair, Aurora felt exactly what her doctor had been encouraging. She felt totally relaxed.

And happy.

Happier than she'd felt in a very, very long time.

9

Aurora awoke and was, at once, completely confused and completely clear. She knew exactly whose shoulder her cheek was resting on. Without even opening her eyes she knew that was Dante's chest hair under her palm, his hand firmly on her ass. But what she didn't understand was how the hell she'd ended up here.

She never slept over. Even on their first night together, she'd waited until he'd fallen asleep and snuck out. After that, he'd made sure she couldn't sneak out, but she'd still managed to kiss him goodnight and leave before the sun was ever close to rising. But here she was, morning sun kissing her closed eyelids, blanket pulled damn near up to her chin.

She pulled away from him and sat up, pushing her hair back from her face. She was dressed in a big, soft t-shirt and sweatpants, her coral dress hanging on a hanger on the back of the closet door.

"You fell asleep during the movie," Dante said in a

low voice, gruff from sleep. "I didn't want to wake you."

Aurora turned and whatever she'd been about to say dried right up in her throat. Dante laid there, one hand crooked under his head, bare chested, his hair tousled from sleep. His eyes were heavy and his stubble was darker than she'd ever seen it.

"Wow." She couldn't help but reach out and touch his sandpapery chin. "Man, you're really handsome."

Dante's eyes lit with so much surprise and delight that it made Aurora realize how rarely she ever complimented him.

"It can't be a shock to hear that, Dante. You know you're attractive."

He gathered her closer, nuzzling his face into her neck and hair. "Sure. I know what I think of myself. But I didn't know what you thought."

She rolled her eyes. "Please, you think I'd have been fucking your brains out all this time if I wasn't attracted to you?" She turned to him, traced one finger over his strong brow, up along the wavy hair at his forehead. "Not to inflate your ego, but you are really, really beautiful."

To Aurora's utter delight, a faint color came into Dante's cheeks. His eyes fell away from hers. "Come on."

"You're embarrassed." She couldn't stop the grin that spread across her face like fire. "I can't believe I figured out how to embarrass Dante Callaghan."

"I'm not. And I'm not that."

"Beautiful or embarrassed? Because from where I'm sitting, you're very much both."

Dante pursed his lips and opened them to say something but his bedroom door burst open.

"Coco, can we do scram-damn-ble this morning? I'm really hungry and... Oh! Aurora! You stayed!"

Aurora's heart completely stopped as a tousle-headed Michelle came marching into Dante's bedroom. Oh crap. Double crap. Triple crap. They hadn't covered any of this. It hadn't even occurred to Aurora that she was going to have to face Michelle this morning. And it definitely hadn't occurred to her that Dante was going to have to explain why Aurora had slept in his bed.

"I'm so glad you're still here!" Michelle jumped up onto the bed with them without hesitation. "Dante never has girls sleep over. Can we check my crystal? Are you staying for breakfast? Dante will make you scram-damn-ble."

Aurora turned to Dante. "Scram-damn-ble?" she asked faintly.

He scrubbed a hand over his face, looking very much like he was trying to keep himself from smiling. "It's just an egg scramble. But I make it so damn good you have to call it a scram-damn-ble."

Aurora looked from Dante's easy, smiling face to Michelle's hopeful grin and she felt something fly right out of her chest. It was almost like letting go of a kite in the wind. She was just tired of clinging to it. And there was no fighting it anymore. She let go of it and wasn't even sad to see it fly away.

She hadn't planned on this. God. She certainly hadn't

planned on this. But while she was here, she was going to enjoy it.

* * *

Dante watched Aurora's face carefully. He knew she'd been shocked when Michelle had just pranced right in. And actually, Dante had been a little surprised himself. It wasn't unusual for Michelle to barge through the house, but he'd thought he'd have another hour or so before she woke up. As he'd lain awake that morning, Aurora sleeping across his chest, he'd been going through his options, including the best way to tell Michelle that Aurora had slept over.

In a different world, he'd have wanted to talk to her about it way before it even happened. But then both of them had fallen asleep during the movie and he hadn't wanted to wake either of them. Aurora sleeping over was a surprise all around and Dante was just relieved that Michelle was taking it so well. She didn't seem to find it weird in the least.

So now, all he could do was roll with the punches and help Aurora do the same. She just looked so damned cute, so different from her usual, immaculate business attire. Her hair was all tumbly and the sleeves of his t-shirt went way past her elbows. She was looking back and forth between him and Michelle like she could barely believe what the hell was going on.

Mildly concerned that Aurora was freaking out, Dante

reached across the bed and grabbed Michelle by the ankle. She laughed and wriggled around as he dragged her across his lap. "Hey, nosy Mcgee. Go get the scram-damn-ble stuff out of the fridge and Aurora and I will be down in a second."

"Okay!" Michelle was up like a shot.

"Oh! And press the button on the coffee maker."

"You got it!" she called over her shoulder.

"Oh! And later today we're going to go over the fundamentals of knocking. Don't worry, you're a bright kid. You'll get it down in no time."

Michelle stuck her tongue out at him and scampered out of the room. They heard her running footsteps down the hall and down the stairs.

"I'm so sorry," Aurora turned to him, chagrin in her eyes.

"For what?" Dante ran a hand over her hair.

"For being here where Michelle could see. And not knowing how to explain it to her. I hope she's not traumatized."

Dante raised a wry eyebrow. "She's resilient. I'm sure seeing you with your makeup smudged wasn't quite enough to send her into therapy."

"Oh!" Aurora's hand went right to her eye make up and she was out of the bed instantly.

Dante chuckled to himself when he heard her furiously washing in the sink. And then he lost his breath when she came back out, pink and fresh from washing her face, his t-shirt falling over one of her shoulders.

"You know that's not what I meant. Will she be traumatized from knowing that we slept in the same bed?"

"No," he said, meaning it. Dante reluctantly slid out of bed and slipped past her into the bathroom, putting toothpaste on his own toothbrush and hunting up a new one for her. He handed it to her and popped his own in his mouth, talking around it. "She knows about the birds and the bees. I mean, ideally I would have talked to her about you sleeping over first, asked her permission, but as you could tell, she didn't seem too bothered by the idea."

Aurora spit toothpaste into the sink, her eyes narrowing. "You would have asked her permission to have me sleep over here?"

He shrugged, splashing water on his face and considering a quick shave. "Sure. It's her house as much as it is mine. And she has to ask me if she wants somebody to sleep over. Makes sense for it to go the other way. Of course, if she said no, we'd have to have a pretty serious conversation about why. But I don't think she would have said no. She obviously likes you."

Deciding against the shave, he turned from the mirror and finally caught Aurora's eye.

"You're a good dad," she said.

He felt the conflict of pleasure and irritation inside him. Pleasure at the praise and irritation at the wording.

"I'm a good brother," he corrected.

She cocked her head at him before going back out to the main room and grabbing her dress off the hook. He sat on the bed and watched her as she slipped out of his clothes and into the dress. So graceful. So gorgeous. Good lord, he could watch this woman do her taxes and he'd still be aroused.

"You don't consider yourself to be her father?"

Dante rose, swiped the t-shirt she'd been wearing off the ground and pulled it over his head. He got instant wood from the scent of it, a combination of him and her. "No. I'm her brother. She has a father. It's just her bad luck that he's a piece of shit."

He didn't want to shut her out or shut her down, but he also really didn't want to go further into this. He knew that she was still teetering on the edge of whether to like him or not and he didn't particularly feel like dragging his daddy issues into the room right now.

Stepping up behind her, he zipped her into her dress. He turned her, and seeing that she was about to say something further about the dad thing, he traced his fingers through the lacy holes at the neck of the dress.

"You know, the way this dress is cut, it makes the skin underneath look like a necklace." He dropped his head and kissed along the delicate cuts of the dress. "A mouthwatering, golden, warm little necklace."

Aurora's sucked in a breath. Dante was completely shocked when suddenly, her soft hands grabbed him firmly on either side of his face. She hauled him toward her and started kissing the daylights out of him. Soft and hard at the same time. Her lips were so lush that no kiss could ever be too hard, but she was using all the force she could muster.

It was intoxicating to Dante.

And confusing as hell.

"I'm waaaaaaiting!" Michelle hollered up the stairs, and Dante and Aurora broke the kiss on a laugh.

He watched as she walked out of the room. He wanted desperately to grab her hand, make her tell him exactly what had her kissing him like that, but he didn't. The moment passed, and all he could do was follow her downstairs.

* * *

Turned out scram-damn-bles were flippin' delicious. But as she'd already insisted he was beautiful and a good dad that morning, Aurora kept her thoughts on his cooking skills to herself. She didn't want to go playing all her cards right now. She was still in shock that she even had those cards to play. Her feelings had come out of nowhere. Blindsided her.

The three of them sat around the breakfast table eating and Michelle held up her newly cleansed crystal, ticking it back and forth on the chain like a pendulum.

"Aurora?"

"Hmmm?"

"Can crystals heal my Von Willebrand's?"

Aurora swallowed what was in her mouth and took a quick second. She could feel Dante's tension from across the table. She didn't have to look at him to know what he was wanting her to say.

"No, they can't, Michelle," Aurora said quietly but firmly, not wanting to crush the little girl or give her false hope. "Remember how I said that they're not magic? They're good for you the way a full night's sleep is good for you, or drinking enough water. They can soothe you or make you feel better, but they don't do miracles."

Michelle cast her eyes down but she nodded. It was the answer she'd been expecting.

"Besides," Dante chipped in. "You know that Von Willebrand's is genetic, Michelle. There's no cure."

"I know. I know." She propped her head on her chin and took a big bite of her eggs. "I guess I just get sick of having it sometimes. I just wish there was more stuff we could do to get rid of it."

"Yeah, that's how I feel about being so dang handsome all the time," Dante said, immediately making Michelle snort and fight a smile. Which, of course, had been the intended effect. "Sometimes it's just such a burden. Every guy wants to be you, every girl wants to get next to you. It's just like, enough already!"

Aurora and Michelle rolled their eyes at each other and laughed. But as Aurora finished off her breakfast, a thought was brewing. One she didn't want to share with Michelle until after she'd shared it with Dante.

10

"You sound like a woman in love," a voice said from behind Aurora as she washed her hands in the sink of the women's bathroom at work the next Monday morning.

Aurora turned and found herself face to face with Rose. She gulped. "I'm sorry?"

"Oh," Rose waved her hand in the air. "None of my business, I'm being nosy. It's just any woman who hums to herself, with that expression on her face, while she washes her hands at work, has got to be in love."

Aurora's eyes went to the mirror and she caught sight of the expression she was making. Well. Shit. There it was. In every line of her face.

Aurora cleared her throat. "I don't know about that." She paused. Decided to tell the truth. "But I certainly had a good weekend."

Rose grinned at her, her auburn hair seeming to light the air around her. "I had one of those myself."

Aurora waited for the plummeting dip of her stomach at the news that Gio and Rose had had a good, presumably sex-filled, weekend together, but it didn't come. Actually, at the moment, Aurora didn't think anything could turn her stomach. She felt like she was walking on air.

"So, who's the guy?" Rose asked, washing her hands herself.

Aurora swallowed hard when Dante's face immediately swam in her mind. She braced a hand against the sink as she felt a little dizzy. Standing there in the women's restroom, two feet from Gio's girlfriend, not only was Aurora not feeling jealous, but she realized, with a kind of dizzy fascination, she'd barely thought of Gio at all the last few weeks. At least not as anything more than a friend and business associate. Rose had asked if she was in love, asked who the guy was, and both times, Aurora's mind went instantly to Dante.

She ran her hand under the cold water and discreetly slipped some onto the back of her neck. When the hell had that happened? Aurora knew that her feelings for Dante were blossoming. That was undeniable. But since when had Dante completely bumped Gio off her radar?

"Aurora?"

Aurora shook her head and focused on Rose. "Sorry?"

"No, that's okay, you just look a little faint, is all. I asked a question and you didn't even hear."

Rose took Aurora by the arm, with a much firmer grip than Aurora expected, and sat her gently on the bench along the wall. "You're looking a little peaked. Do you feel alright? I'm a nurse."

Aurora smoothed her hair back. "I'm alright. I'm just a little dizzy from the pregnancy is all."

"You're pregnant?" The sweet look of delight on Rose's face was undeniable.

"Oh. Crap." Aurora held one hand over her mouth. "I didn't mean to say that out loud. I'm pregnant, but I haven't told anyone yet. Including the father."

Rose immediately zipped her lips. "I won't say a word. I promise. Can I get you anything? Seltzer? Juice? A cookie?"

Aurora rubbed a hand over her belly. "Apparently the baby likes the sound of all three of those things."

The two women laughed. Just as she'd expected she would that night at the fundraiser, Aurora genuinely liked Rose. What the hell was going on here? Her life was changing faster than she could even keep track of.

"I heard your question before," Aurora said. "About who the guy is. I just, I got a little surprised because the answer wasn't what I thought it was going to be."

Rose cocked her head to one side and leaned up against the sink. "Again, not my business, but you're in love with two people?"

Aurora shook her head. "No. No, not anymore, apparently. But it seems I *am* in love. I just didn't realize it until now." She put her hand over her belly again. "Oh lord. What am I going to do?"

"I know we don't know each other very well, Aurora," Rose started, biting her bottom lip between her teeth. "But can I give you a little advice?"

"Sure."

"Did you know that Gio and I knew each other in high school?"

"Oh?" Aurora's brow furrowed. She'd had no idea.

"Yeah. And things fell apart right after graduation. And, you know, that was that. But fifteen years later, it turns out that wasn't exactly that, you know what I mean?"

"Ah. No. Not really."

Rose grinned. "Sorry, I know this isn't making a ton of sense. Look. I guess I'll just say that when you know, you know. And all you can do is get out of your own way. People fall out of love all the time. But if there's one thing I know, it's that you sure can't make yourself un-love somebody. No matter how hard you try. It's useless. So if you feel it, you might as well show it."

* * *

Dante leaned back in his desk chair and scraped a hand over his stubble. He held the phone away from his ear for a second, just to get a break from Gio's voice. He was making sense, but damn if he didn't annoy the ever-loving crap out of Dante these days.

He'd never had a problem working with Gio in the past, even if the two of them were very different people with very different views on how things should get done. But these days, Dante felt his fuse get shorter and shorter with the man.

Aurora was between them. And as far as Dante could tell, Gio didn't even know that Aurora was between them. The man didn't even know that Aurora was pining for him. And Dante was fairly certain she was. She never mentioned him, looked so uncomfortable if he was mentioned, and she'd been coming over to see Dante more and more often. For the hundredth time, Dante cursed himself for ever proposing the idea that she use him to get over Gio.

He'd thought that having Aurora in any way, at any cost, would be better than not having her at all. But lately, knowing that she really wanted Gio was driving him insane. It never affected him when he and Aurora were together. When she was there in front of him, touching him or kissing him, Dante didn't think twice about it. All he could think was how perfect she was, how much he wanted her. But then later, he'd think back on it. And he'd realize that she'd probably been picturing Gio the entire time they were together. Every time it felt like a poison spreading through his body.

It was almost like he couldn't get a moment alone with her. There were always three people in the room: Aurora, Dante, and the ghost of Giovanni Esposito.

He fucking hated it. But his only option was to put up with it, or break things off with her.

That was never happening. Not when he could barely stand to go the few days she always made him wait between phone calls. Between hook ups. He never called her, didn't want to pressure her. And besides, that wasn't the way their arrangement worked.

He thought back on their weekend together. He was grateful to Michelle being so dang pushy. Because it meant that Aurora had stayed over Saturday night as well. And on Sunday, the three of them had gone to a movie, ordered more food.

But now it was Monday and while he'd gone to bed with Aurora in his arms, he'd woken up completely alone. No phone call. No text. No thanks for the weekend. Nothing. Just like that first night they'd hooked up.

It had pissed him off. And it had meant that he'd argued with Michelle over every little thing and ensured that he'd sent her off to school in just as bad a mood as he was in.

Now it was halfway through Monday and his mood had only worsened. Aurora still hadn't called or texted and as far as Dante was concerned, all of it was the fault of the man on the other end of the line right now.

"I think we should be able to have the specs on the Peterson project in another week. But it depends on whatever happens on your end," Gio said. "Are you close to sealing the deal there?"

"Of course I am. What do I look like, an amateur?" Dante snapped and couldn't help the wave of pleasure he got from being an asshole to Gio.

Gio sighed. "God, you're touchy these days. No. You aren't an amateur, Dante. But you have been off your game recently and it's not ridiculous for me to check in here. Between you and Aurora, I swear, it's like tiptoeing through mousetraps."

That had Dante's ears perking up. "What's that? Aurora's been in a bad mood recently?"

Gio was quiet for a minute. "Not a bad mood exactly, but she's been colder than usual, I guess. I mean, you know her. She's uber professional. But she's always been warm with me. And that's not really there recently. I must have done something to piss her off."

Music to Dante's fucking ears. She wasn't being as warm to Gio as she usually was? What the hell was he supposed to make of that? He figured it could mean one of two things. One, she was just pissed that Gio had found someone else and she was trying to keep herself from getting hurt again. Or two, her more tender feelings were currently being expended somewhere else, or on someone else.

The thought had Dante losing his breath. Suddenly in a much better mood than he'd been in all day, he found himself much less irritated with Gio and much less anxious to end the call.

"Any word from Raphael DePella?" Dante asked, referring to a client that he and Gio had been trying to land for months.

"Yes, actually. Hold on, I'll forward you the email he sent me from Greece."

"Greece? He's still on that fucking vacation?"

"Yeah, I'm not sure he's in the mood to talk business anytime soon which is a shame because…

Gio's voice faded away as the door to Dante's office

opened and there was Aurora. One hand on the knob and one hand pulling her messenger bag off and tossing it on the floor. She wore a silky lavender blouse and a cream colored pencil skirt. Her blonde hair was in a long, thick braid over one of her shoulders. And she had a look in her eye that Dante had come to know and love quite a bit.

She'd come here to scratch an itch.

Dante watched, the phone still to his ear, as she closed the door behind her and locked it. He watched as she stepped purposefully across his office, her hips swaying and her eyes heated.

Dante could hear Gio's voice in his ear, but he couldn't for the life of him understand a word the man was saying. He made a non committal sound in the back of his throat hoping it sounded like he was still listening.

And then Aurora was standing there, in front of him, looking perfect and untouchable and as gorgeous as always. Dante's mouth watered. He patted his lap, asking her to climb on, but she shook her head.

Bending down, she clamped a hand onto Dante's knee and swiveled his chair so that he was facing her. Standing between his legs, Aurora's eyes burned into his. She kept eye contact as she slowly bent down in front of him, going to her knees.

Dante's mouth instantly dried up. He pulled the phone away from his ear. "Sweetheart," he murmured, but she shook her head, pushed the phone back toward his ear and dropped her eyes to his belt.

She wanted him to keep the phone call going?

Aurora made quick work of his belt and the zipper of his pants. Within seconds she was holding his cock, huge and hot in her hand. She'd never gone down on him before but now she was looking at him as if she wanted to devour him whole.

"Sure, yeah. That makes sense," Dante said into the phone, his voice tight.

Leaning forward, Aurora didn't waste any more time. She held him steady in one hand and swallowed him down.

Dante widened his legs and planted his feet and did everything he could not to jam his cock down her throat. But she was not making it easy. He wasn't prepared for the way her luscious lips looked closing around him. He wasn't prepared for the alluring peek down her blouse she was giving him. He wasn't prepared for the vicious little circles she was making with her tongue.

She was going to drive him insane. And, shit, she was going to make him come. But he wasn't nearly ready for that.

* * *

God, he tasted good, Aurora thought. Clean and warm and salty. She didn't think she would ever get enough of his flavor. She swirled her tongue around the head and took him deep again.

Dante's hips pushed up, seemingly of their own accord, and he flexed involuntarily in her mouth. Aurora held back a feline smile. It wouldn't do to be smug at a moment like this, but she could tell she was taking him apart, piece by piece.

"Fuck," Dante bit out. "Ah. No. Never mind."

He was still on the phone and the thought of it was so hot to Aurora that she was already completely soaked through her panties. His free hand threaded through her hair and Aurora was as aroused by the pressure he put on the back of her head as she was by the tender way his fingers stroked at her scalp. She sucked him off for several wondrous minutes as he grew more and more intense. At one point, he tightened his hold on her hair, tried to pull her off of him. She sucked him in harder, farther down her throat.

* * *

Dante grunted, his eyes crossing at the sensations ricocheting through his body. Gio spoke in his ear again and the sound of that fucker's voice suddenly enraged Dante. He looked down at the top of Aurora's gorgeous head.

Was she acting out some erotic scenario that she had dreamed about doing to Gio? Was this on her bucket list? Was she still trying to bang Gio out of her system? It was something he could have ignored if not for the fact that Gio was fucking talking in his ear at that very second.

It sent the blood screaming through his body and broke something deep inside Dante. Whatever leash he'd been using to hold himself back snapped. He pulled Aurora off of him and stood, dragging her to her feet.

Fuck this shit.

Dante nearly smashed his phone in his grip. With his free hand, he flipped Aurora around so that she was bent over his desk. He grabbed the hem of her skirt and hauled it up over her hips. The white lace of her thong glowed against her golden skin and Dante yanked it out of the way.

"Yes," she moaned quietly, the heat of her breath fogging the glossy finish of his desk as she laid her cheek on it.

He didn't think anymore. There were no thoughts. There was only instinct. There was only need.

With Gio's voice still buzzing in his ear, Dante reared back and pressed himself fully into Aurora, stretching her to the extreme. He knew it was just on the edge of pain and pleasure for her by the way she flexed and stretched her hands on the edge of the desk.

Dante held himself still, letting her acclimate, and then he reached forward and placed his palm around her mouth, keeping her moans inside. He might be willing to secretly fuck her with Gio on the phone. But he sure as hell wasn't willing to let Gio hear her pleasure. Hell no. That was for Dante and Dante alone.

He pulled back and then slammed back into her wetness. Aurora's back arched, her legs trembled, and he felt her mouth open against his palm.

And just like that, he didn't give a fuck about Gio

anymore. He had his hands full of Aurora and the only thing he could do was share his passion with her. The only thing he could do was to love her the only way she would let him.

"I can't fucking talk right now, Gio," he snapped into the phone and pressed end on the call, tossing the device away. He froze for a second. Shit, he shouldn't have said Gio's name. He gave it away. What if it took her out of the moment? Or worse, what if she was thinking about Gio now.

He thrust himself forward, almost savagely, and Aurora tore her mouth from his hand. She turned her head and looked him full in the eye.

During sex she was usually hazy, her eyes blurry and unfocused, but here she was, staring right through him. It sent a white hot thrill through Dante. She couldn't be thinking of someone else when she was looking him in the eye. She could only be thinking of him. Of what he was doing to her. Of the pleasure he was giving to her. No one else. Just her. He plunged into her with the ferocity and speed of an animal. He was lost in her heat, in the tight squeeze of her. He could have died happy right then.

He felt her tighten around him, watched her face tense and release with her pleasure as her fingertips gripped the edge of the desk.

He slipped his hand around to her front and worked her clit through her orgasm, prolonging it as much as he could. He could have sworn that she came twice.

But then her orgasm tugged his right out of him. He

was rutting her, claiming her. He tangled his hand in her braid and her head came up off the desk as he tugged back. She was bowed for him, accepting everything he gave her, and he gave her everything. Every ounce of liquid pleasure was rung out of him as he rode her through it.

And then there was nothing to do but collapse over her back, kiss along her neck and over the shell of her ear.

"Baby," he whispered to her, sliding one arm around her to hug her as tight as he could. "Jesus, baby. Sweetheart. You gorgeous girl. You perfect, luscious goddess. God, you undid me. Tore me apart." He continued whispering in her ear until she chuckled.

"Guess you liked it, huh?"

"I saw the white light. Almost went through the pearly gates on that one, sweetheart." Dante reached between them to grab the base of the condom he always wore when he realized in a heart stopping moment that there was no condom.

He pulled out anyways, grabbed her hand, and dragged her into the adjoining bathroom. He closed the door behind them, wetted some paper towel and fell to his knees in front of her, gently cleaning her up.

"Sweetheart," he started, unsure on how to proceed. Better just go whole hog. Tell the damn truth. "I forgot to put on a condom."

"Shit," she murmured reflexively. Then she reached out and smoothed his furrowed brow. "We both forgot."

That soothed a bit of his guilt, but it didn't soothe the panic racing through him. "I'm clean, got tested just before we slept together the first time and you're the only one I've been with since then."

Now Aurora was the one furrowing her brow, as if she almost didn't believe that he hadn't been man whoring around Los Angeles. "Me too. I'm clean."

Dante put her underwear back in place and pulled her skirt down, smoothing out the wrinkles. Rising, he took her hands in his. His heart was in his throat. "Could I have gotten you pregnant?"

Aurora's face instantly went flat, and a careful expression came over it. She cleared her throat. "No."

So she was on birth control of some kind. Dante let out a deep breath. "Thank god. That could have been really bad." He let his hands trail down her shoulders and bent to kiss her lips, unaware of the flash of mortal pain that stabbed across her features at his words. "You just got me so revved up, I couldn't even think straight. That's never happened to me before."

She cleared her throat again and raised an eyebrow as she turned to wash her hands in the sink. "You've never gotten head before?"

He laughed. "No, I mean I've never gone bareback before."

"Really?" She looked at him with complete disbelief.

Feathers ruffled, he reached around her to wash his own hands. "Sometimes your low opinion of me gets a little old, Aurora. I'm not Hugh fucking Hefner. So I've dated a lot. Who hasn't? But I don't lie. And I'm telling you I've never fucked a woman without a condom."

Aurora took a step back from him, dried her hands on a towel and tossed it into the trash. "Okay."

She was opening the door to the bathroom when he slammed a hand on it to keep her from leaving. "That's all you have to say about that?"

In a move that was extremely out of character with the polished, ladylike exterior, Aurora slapped his hand right off the door.

She spun around, one finger directly in his face. "You obviously have your panties all in a twist over something, Callaghan. But trust me, you don't want to get into it with me."

And then she was striding out of the bathroom, leaving him to stare at every graceful, Amazonian inch of her. He barely got in front of her before she could exit his office. "I'm sorry. I'm being a total ass and I'm sorry. But you're being a little bit of an ass too."

She stepped back, cocked out one hip and folded her arms across her chest, raised an eyebrow.

"And," Dante continued, "while I'm trying hard to be mad at you for being an ass and thinking the worst of me, you're so mad right now that your New Orleans accent is finally coming out and turns out I find that really cute."

Aurora's hands dropped from over her chest and fell to her sides. "Oh. Well, I tried to lose it during business school but sometimes it creeps back in."

Knowing that the irritated heat between them was on a low simmer right now, Dante hedged his bets and stepped forward, slipping his hand over her golden hair.

"I don't know why you'd try to lose it. It's beautiful. Makes you sound like a Georgia peach."

At that, Aurora threw her head back and laughed. "Trust me when I say I am not that at all. And no New Orleans girl wants to be called that. We're in our own category, baby."

And Dante just said, "Abso-fucking-lutely you are."

11

"Lunch," Dante said a minute later, taking her hand and dragging her from the office.

Aurora couldn't help but glance back at his desk, all cluttered and messy from where he'd just bent her over it. She couldn't believe she'd just stormed into his office and devoured him. And with Gio on the other end of the line! It somehow made her feel both proud and horrified.

"It's four o'clock in the afternoon, Dante."

"Happy hour drinks, then. I just don't want you to go yet. Come out with me, Aurora. We don't even have to call it a date."

Her stomach flipped, as it so often did these days. She wasn't sure if it was from the baby growing inside her or from the idea of going on a real date with Dante.

"Coffee," she finally said.

Ten minutes later, they settled themselves at a small cafe a few blocks from Dante's office.

"Want to play a game?" he asked.

"Um, I thought we already did," she said with a smile.

He laughed. "You're right. And it's my favorite game of all. But for the sake of variety, let's play a different kind this time. One I used to do with Michelle all the time."

"What is it?"

"It was something we did when she wanted to be a detective. I called up this guy I knew in college who ended up being a P.I. and he told me the best way to train to be a detective was to observe as much as you could about every person you were with and every place you went. So everywhere she and I went, we played the observation game. For like a full year. By the end, it sort of became second nature. But then she got into her Harry Potter phase and it all went down the drain."

"You didn't call up a wizard you knew in college to give her some tips on harnessing magic?" Aurora asked dryly. Although inside she was quaking, stunned at the sweetness inside him. He'd called up a P.I. for career tips because his little sister wanted to be a detective. It was almost painful it was so cute.

Dante shrugged. "So you wanna play?"

"The observation game?" Aurora looked around, taking in the doilies on the tables and the geriatric clientele. "Sure."

"Not about the place though, just about one another."

"Oh. You want me to tell you what I observe about you?"

"And vice versa. I'm pretty sure I already know what you think about me, but let's give it a shot."

143

"Alright." She smoothed her hair back in a nervous gesture. "You go first."

"There are two Aurora LeMondes."

"What?"

He leaned back in his chair, his large hands spread on the delicate table cloth, his coffee cooling in front of him. His eyes were so blue in that moment, Aurora swore they made her thirsty. "There's the woman that I've known for years. The version of you that works at the Esposito Group. Polished, calm, never misses a deadline. Deadly beautiful, of course, but you keep it behind a glass case. Like the rose in Beauty and the Beast. I didn't know why, but I knew that the polished version of you wasn't the whole picture. And I thought, why is she hiding? But now I get it."

Aurora took a sip of tea, trying to keep her hand from quaking on the cup. He was freakishly accurate so far. She didn't trust her voice so she said nothing.

"It's because you have to keep the other part of you under wraps. I got a glimpse of her every time I would flirt with you and it would annoy you. I'd see just a little bit of the spice. The temper. The flare of heat. But I wasn't prepared. I had no idea what it would be like when you finally raised the gates and let it loose. The night you asked me to take you home? I'll never forget it. Part of me is still recovering. It was like pressing my tongue to a battery. The other part of you, the other version, is so passionate, so fiery, so free and wild, that you have to keep her in the cage. Or else nobody will ever get any work done."

She took another sip of tea. "I don't know if that's true. But…my first year of college, I had not one, but two married professors try to hook up with me."

Dante's brow instantly furrowed. She didn't miss the way his hand balled on the table.

She shrugged it off though. "My body, my nature, it all worked against me. No matter how smart I was or the grades I got or the ideas I had, it was all liable to go down the drain the second I got labeled a slut. I realized that the only way to rise in the business world was to become an ice queen. Untouchable, as you called it."

"Except for your crooked teeth," he quipped, making her smile just as he intended.

"Right. I knew I should have sprung for the Invisalign." She sighed and looked out the window for a second. "The ambition I have to survive in the business world isn't just for personal satisfaction. It isn't a game. For me and my mother, my job is a matter of survival."

He almost interrupted, but she opened her mouth again, her eyes blurry as she watched her own finger play in a ring of condensation left behind by her tea cup. "You know, I think it became even worse when I started at Esposito. The cold and polished version of me intensified, crystallized. Gio recognized my talent right away, but part of me was so worried that I'd slip up and he'd see the other part of me. The part that spent the first eight years of my life in shelters while my mother sold fortunes on corners for five bucks a pop. The part of me that never knew my father and secretly had absolutely no idea how to talk to men. The part of me that every once in a while, lost her shit and had to find a man to let loose on. I was so scared that Gio would see that part of me that I locked her away, never to be seen or heard from again."

* * *

Dante was riveted. Absorbing every piece of information from her like it was the coolest, cleanest water. He hadn't realized how thirsty he'd been to know her. Her story was hard to hear but he wanted to know more. He wanted all of it.

"Well," he said, sliding his hand across the table to hers, a little smile on his face. "Maybe not 'never'. She's been known to come over to my house a few nights a week."

Aurora smiled down into her tea. "Fair enough."

He paused for a second, and then decided to do what his intuition told him to do. "When you say shelters, you mean homeless shelters?"

Aurora gave him a sad little smile then nodded. "Yeah. My mom is a free spirit in a lot of ways and she wasn't planning on getting pregnant with me. She was young."

Aurora turned to look out the window, watch the pedestrians pass by as she told her story. The afternoon light slanted across her face and lit her hazel eyes from the side, making them look like a glass bottle. Dante had the sudden urge to take her to the beach. Somewhere tropical where she could full-out lay in the sun. Take that full, deep breath she never quite seemed able to take.

"She'd been couch surfing, I guess. Which isn't too much of a hardship at age twenty. But then she was plus one and a lot of those couches were suddenly occupied. She had a few friends who stuck it out with her. But we were often in shelters." She straightened her top suddenly, as if she was having to remind herself that she was here, now, a successful woman, not the vulnerable child she'd once been. "It wasn't as bad for me. When you're a kid, you don't really know what's going on. And I always had her there with me, so I always felt safe. She was a fierce protector. But it must have been terrible for her."

"God." Dante tried to imagine what that would have felt like with Michelle. "I'll bet she barely ever slept. I know I wouldn't have if Michelle and I were in that position."

Aurora looked at him for a minute, her eyes inscrutable x-rays.

"What changed?" Dante asked. "How did you get back on your feet?"

"My mother started taking a few courses that they offered at one of the community centers we used to go to for dinners sometimes. She got just enough under her belt that she made a fairly decent secretary. She did that for a while at some accounting office. It was enough to put us into a little apartment and give us health insurance. One of the accountants started to get a little handsy, so she moved on to a therapist's office. But pretty soon, the clientele started talking more to my mother about their problems than they were to the therapist."

"Because of all the witchy stuff?"

Aurora smiled. "Because my mother sees a lot of things other people don't. And it makes her pretty easy to talk   to."

"Let me guess, the therapist fired her out of jealousy?"

"The opposite, in fact. The therapist was very impressed with her. Fired her as a secretary and renovated this big old coat closet to be her office."

"Her office for what?"

"Fortune telling, advice, aura readings. It all sounds so mystical, and a lot of clients thought it was hooey. But there's plenty of people in New Orleans who need occult help with their lives. And not only is my mother the real deal when it comes to that kind of thing, but she also wasn't trying to squeeze every dollar out of every client's pocket. She really wanted to use her gifts to help people."

He leaned forward, loving how open she was being. Wanting even more from her. "Do you have any of those gifts?"

"Not nearly as potent. But probably more than you do."

He nodded slowly, leaning back. "Can you predict the future?"

Aurora snorted. "Of course not."

"Can you, like, see my aura?"

Aurora raised one eyebrow. "Dante, I can see your

aura from fifty paces."

"You're kidding."

She   shrugged.
"You're not kidding?"

She shrugged again.

"Come on. Tell me! What color is my aura?"

"As red as the day is long."

"Really?" Dante held up one hand in front of his face as if he could look hard enough and see it for himself.

Aurora bit her lip. "People with red auras are very physical. Sexual. Grounded in the here and now. They believe in what they can taste and feel and see. They're stubborn. They think they know how the world works. They're passionate yet practical. Successful."

Dante found himself clearing his throat. "Well. I guess that sounds about right."

"The aura reading didn't count as my turn for the observation game."

"Okay. Your turn then." Dante shrugged, seemingly casual, but his heart rate had definitely picked up.

Now it was Aurora's turn to lean back in her chair. Dante refused to shift in his seat. "You're a natural caretaker. But you're uncomfortable with that idea because you view yourself as a survivor, selfish even. But you're not. The furthest thing from it, actually. You protect the people you care about. Even nurture them. You're good at it. It comes naturally to you. But it also comes naturally to you to be a dick. Top dog."

Dante laughed. "You flatter me."

Aurora cocked her head to one side. "You don't like Gio. You two were never best friends, but now you can barely stand to be in the same room as him."

"Do you blame me? He has your heart, after all."

* * *

At Dante's bold words, Aurora practically jerked in her seat. But why was she so surprised. Of course he'd think that. She'd never taken Dante's proposal seriously, to fuck Gio out of her system by using him. She hadn't ever thought that would be possible. She'd just been hungry for Dante himself. But now, looking into Dante's deep blue eyes, remembering his intensity when he'd fucked her across the desk as he'd been on the phone with Gio, she realized that Dante still thought that's why she'd been with him over the last few weeks.

She didn't want to deliberately mislead Dante, but considering her main reason for starting anything with him, in addition to her desire of course, had involved being pregnant with a child he didn't want, Aurora wasn't sure she should relieve him of the misconception yet. She certainly wasn't ready to tell him she thought she was falling in love with him.

"It was your idea, Dante." She spoke in a soft tone.

He looked away from her, then.

Sometimes she just didn't understand him. He cared about her, she was sure of it. But she still had absolutely no idea how he'd react to her having his kid. Oh, she was sure that she could trust him not to force her into anything she didn't want. And despite what he'd said about not wanting kids, she was sure she could count on him for financial support. But she wasn't sure he'd still want to be with her. What if he wanted to end things? What if he simply said thanks, but no thanks, and wished her luck? She wasn't sure her fragile, hormonal heart could take it. She'd grown used to his affection for her. Depended on it. Needed it.

She didn't know what to do!

But maybe if she introduced Dante to her mother, her mother could help her decide.

"Dante, do you want to meet my mother?" The words were out of her mouth before she could stop them.

"Really?"

Aurora cleared her throat. "It's not a big deal. She's a casual person."

"Sure. I just thought you wanted this thing between us to be more… secret than that."

Well, she had. At the beginning. But now she was all tangled up, totally confused, had no idea which way was up. And she needed to call in the big guns. "I've met Michelle." She shrugged. "You should meet my mother. Unless you don't want to."

"No, I want to. I mean, I'd be lying if I said I wasn't nervous to meet a practicing witch…"

Aurora rolled her eyes. "I'm not going through this with you again. My mother is not a witch."

"You only say that because if she's a witch then you

have to admit you're a witch too."

Aurora bit back her smile. "If I was a witch, I would have cast an expulsion charm against you a long time ago."

"Ah, that was back when you didn't like me. I'm not so worried about that these days."

But he was worried, she thought. She saw it in his eyes, his lingering unease about her feelings for Gio. Oh, Dante, she thought, if you only knew. I love you. I love our child.

I just want you to love the both of us too.

12

A week after having coffee with Dante, Aurora pulled into her mother's driveway, Dante jammed into the front seat of her Honda Civic.

She grinned at the way his long legs were folded up in front of him. He made it look like a clown car. But even in that ridiculous position he was devastatingly handsome. He wore dark jeans and a deep blue sweater, the same color as his eyes. He'd also gotten a haircut that week and his hair was as short as it was the first time they'd hooked up. Aurora couldn't help but shiver as she remembered what it had felt like against her hand as she tried to grip him there. The masculine scrape of his short hair against her palm.

"What?" he asked her, undoing his seatbelt. "I have something on my face?"

"No," she said, lifting her hand to caress the stubble on his chin. "You look just the way you did that first night we were together, with your hair so short."

"Oh yeah." He raked a hand over his hair and smiled at the memory of that night.

"You looked so severe in that suit and short hair. All shadows and sharp angles. Have I ever told you that sometimes you can suck all the air out of a room?"

He cocked his head to one side, trying to get a read on her mood. "Is that a good thing?"

"It's a *you* thing. Sometimes you're just too much man for one room. It's distracting."

With that, she slid out of the car and heard him follow suit. She was halfway up the brick walkway toward her mother's front door when Dante caught her by the arm and spun her around.

"You like me," he said, a teasing glint in his eyes.

"Excuse me?" She raised an eyebrow.

"All this time, I haven't been sure. You're attracted to me, of course." An arrogant look slid across his features. "But that right there? What just happened. You just gave away your cards. You like me."

"Well, yeah. I should hope that I like the person I've been sleeping with for the last month and a half."

"No," he said, waving away her dismissive words and pulling her close, swiping her smooth fall of hair over her shoulder and taking her by the chin. She would have been a bowl of jelly at his feet if not for the teasing, arrogant glint in his eye that had the steel in her spine stiffening. "It's more than just casual regard. You *like me* like me."

"What are we, in the third grade?"

"Am I interrupting?"

They looked up to see Aurora's mother leaning against the doorjamb of her front house.

"Not at all. You must be Cedalie. I'm Dante Callaghan," Dante said, lightly releasing Aurora and stepping around toward Cedalie, his hand held out.

* * *

Dante was a bit surprised by the older woman's appearance. Very attractive, she barely looked over thirty-five except for the few gossamer strands of silver in her hair. She wore a man's shirt, worn and tucked into old jeans. One of her bare feet was propped up on her knee and Dante could see lots of silver toe rings. Three crystals of various colors hung from her neck.

He held his hand out to her and then paused. "Is it bad luck to shake hands with a witch?" he asked her, only half joking.

Cedalie threw her head back and laughed.

"Yes," she said, stepping toward Dante and hugging him instead. She pulled back and kissed him square on the mouth. A hard kiss, eyes open.

"Bonjou, Manman," Aurora said, stepping into her mother's embrace. "Pa li fe pe."

Don't scare him.

Cedalie grinned and opened the door to them. "Byinvini."

Welcome.

"You speak French, Aurora?" Dante asked in

amazement as he followed the two women into the small bungalow. He was so surprised by this new tidbit of information about her that he barely noticed the crystals swinging from wires, the wind chimes, the bundles of grasses and herbs scattered on the kitchen table, the half dealt deck of tarot cards.

"That's Louisiana Creole, bebe," Cedalie said, patting the side of his face and pushing out a chair at the kitchen table. "I thought you might bring your little one."

Dante swung his attention back to Cedalie, finally taking a minute to look around her house. He opened his mouth to answer, but Cedalie was already talking.

"No, you don't have to make up something about her having a busy schedule. The truth is completely understandable."

"The truth?" Dante asked, a little bemused.

"Sure, bebe. You wanted to check me out first before you brought your little one here. You don't bring her just anywhere. You're a papa bear like that. But by the end of our visit, you'll see that me and she would get along very nice."

"Oh. I...." Dante's eyes slid sideways toward Aurora, looking to her for a gauge on the situation.

"I'm not just guessing that we'd get along well. I know for fact. You might have left her at home, but you bring a little bit of her everywhere you go. I can feel her energy from where you hold it close." Cedalie raised her hand to her lips in the gesture of a lifetime smoker, but dropped it and fished in her pocket for a toothpick. She pointedly ignored the annoyed look her daughter was shooting her way. "She's curious, but realistic. Imaginative but very grounded. She takes care of you as much as you take care of her. She wishes she could play more sports, but you don't let her." Cedalie cocked her head to one side and surveyed Dante. "Why don't you let her?"

"You don't have to answer that, Dante," Aurora said, setting a cup of iced tea in front of him and joining them at the table. "Mama, stop showing off."

"No, that's okay," Dante cleared his throat, recrossed his legs and looked at Cedalie the way he might look at someone across a conference room table. "You can see so much but you can't see the reason I don't let her play sports?"

Cedalie sucked her lips in to keep her smile back, the same as Aurora often did. The familiar gesture immediately softened any prickliness Dante may have felt about being read so thoroughly and immediately by Cedalie. The two of them, equally confident, eyed one another across the table.

"I can see a great deal, although my daughter thinks it's 'rude' and 'totally stalls the conversation' if I don't let people tell me some things for themselves." Cedalie made air quotes, exaggerated enough to have Dante chuckling.

Casually, Dante reached over and laced his fingers with Aurora's. "My sister has a blood disorder that makes sports, especially contact ones, not possible for her. But if you're telling me that she's really pining after it, then maybe I'll have to look into something she could play that doesn't have too much risk."

Cedalie nodded, a small look of chagrin on her face now. "Maybe I was trying to show off a little bit. But I wasn't trying to tell you how to raise your child."

"My sister," Dante corrected automatically. Cedalie's eyes zipped to Aurora's and Aurora immediately looked away.

"Shall we go for a walk?" Aurora suggested.

A few hours later, Dante let out a deep, exaggerated breath in the front seat of Aurora's car as they pulled out of Cedalie's driveway. He slumped dramatically against Aurora's shoulder and she lightly shoved him back, unable to do the same with her smile. "I'm driving! And it wasn't that bad. She lightened up on all the occult stuff after the first twenty minutes or so."

"Yeah, and the rest was just a walk in the park. I loved the part when she made me balance that rock on my head to balance my chakras."

"It was a very small crystal and your chakras really needed cleansing. Trust me."

"That wasn't the craziest part though," Dante insisted. "Your mom is HOT. I thought my eyes were going to bug out of my head when I first saw her. The woman could be your older sister."

"Well, she was only twenty when she had me. She's not much older than you are."

"Oh god. Don't go there. I'm closer to your age than I am to hers."

"Mmhmm."

"I don't have to take this abuse. Drop me off at this bus stop! I'll find my own way home."

"No way, I could never live with myself for treating the elderly that way."

Aurora yelped and laughed as he tugged her in for a kiss. Luckily they were safely stopped at a stoplight.

* * *

A half an hour later, Aurora was on her way home. She'd been so tempted to stay with Dante, and he'd wanted the same thing, but she'd needed some time on her own after the intensity of introducing Dante to Cedalie. And frankly, Aurora really needed to mull over what her mother had pulled her aside to say.

"You have to tell him, child. You have to."

"I'm not ready, Manman. You're the one who told me to wait, to gather information as long as I could."

"That was before. That was before I saw the way he was about his sister. He doesn't want children, child. I can see this plain as day. He's not lying. To you or to himself."

The words had cut through Aurora like a blade through a flower petal.

"But if you wait, the longer you wait, you risk ruining your relationship with him. And I can see what it has come to mean to you."

"What do you mean 'ruin it', Mama? You mean that he'll be mad that I kept it from him for so long?"

Cedalie had paused. She seemed to mull something over in her mind. Aurora knew that look on her mother's face. She'd seen it a hundred times. It was the look Cedalie got when she knew more than she wanted to. *"No. I don't mean that. I can't say more, child. You know that."*

Dante had come out of the bathroom then and there hadn't been much more to say anyway. Her mother was not going to say much more than she already had. Because to speak about it would be to interfere with it, and that was not her mother's place. It never had been. Aurora understood that, but she was also deeply disconcerted over her mother's change of heart.

Aurora pulled into the driveway of her apartment building and parked, hurrying up to her home. She showered quickly and threw on pajamas, needing nothing more than to sink into the oblivion of sleep.

Her head was spinning. Aurora hadn't realized how much comfort she'd been taking from the plan to wait and gather information. Letting things play out little by little. It had allowed her to keep things as they were, and the only thing changing was her level of closeness with Dante. But now her mother was completely flipping the script. Telling Aurora to turn everything on its head. The thought of having that conversation with Dante chilled Aurora down to the bone. She knew that it would change everything. She thought of the way he'd looked today, walking arm in arm with her mother. His t-shirt straining across his chest. The confident little swagger in his hips. God.

She'd tell him and there'd be no more casual dinner

and movie nights with Michelle. She'd tell him and she would lose the right to come knocking whenever her desire for him overwhelmed her. She'd tell him and every time she saw him it would be so awkward that she'd start to dread doing business with him.

Aurora tossed and turned. She wanted the baby and he didn't. And things were bound to get so tense that either she'd have to dissolve her partnership with Gio or Dante would. Everything would go away the minute she told him. And all she'd have left were these memories.

And his baby.

Not for the first time since she'd gotten pregnant, Aurora pressed the flat of her palm over her belly. She closed her eyes and tried, really tried, to feel the life in there. And of course, she instantly did. Aurora's eyes came open. There the baby was. A zipping, growing energy inside of her. Aurora could feel the baby. She could feel her future there.

This baby deserved to come into a world where things were clear and calm between its parents. Aurora didn't think they'd be a classic family. The chances of that went up in smoke the night she'd jumped Dante's bones. But they did have a shot at peace. All she needed to do was tell him. Come clean. That way, they could move on.

She just hoped they could move on together.

13

Dante reached over the back of Michelle's seat in the movie theater to play with a silky strand of Aurora's hair. Aurora turned and gave him a soft little smile. He didn't think she was paying attention to this movie any more than he was.

But Michelle had wanted to come and she'd wanted popcorn and she'd wanted to sit in the middle. None of which she'd demanded but all of which she'd engineered with alarming alacrity. Dante was really going to have trouble on his hands when she was a teenager. Besides the seating arrangements, Dante really had nothing to complain about. Nothing like a movie on a stormy Saturday afternoon with his girls.

His stomach bottomed out for a second before quickly rebounding. It had shocked him the first time he'd realized he was thinking of Michelle and Aurora that way. His girls. But he was slowly getting used to the thought now.

Somehow, over the last two months, Aurora had

worked her way into being a part of his family.

He knew that Michelle was feeling the same way too. She was always disappointed when Aurora didn't sleep over. And she'd started asking Dante questions about marriage, about mothers, and most alarmingly, about whether he'd ever have any kids.

"It'd be cool," she'd said. "I would be an aunt and a sister all at once."

"Why's that?" he'd asked, handing her half of the peanut butter sandwich he'd just made.

"Because you're like my brother and dad all at once, so your kid would be like my sister and niece or brother and nephew all at once. It would be cool."

Michelle had shrugged and hopped down from the counter, ready to get back into whatever she was reading, but Dante had sat, dumbfounded, for another twenty minutes.

He'd always been so careful with Michelle, reminding her over and over that he was her brother, not her dad. He'd kept their father fresh in both their minds. Not in order to honor the man, but as a cautionary tale for both of them. Positions in their family had to be earned, not given without discretion. And their father sure as hell hadn't earned a place in their lives.

Dante had no idea that Michelle was starting to think of him as a dad. It both thrilled and scared the shit out of him at the same time. He could be a brother. He was a hell of a brother. But father? He had no idea how to do that. None at all. He supposed that it probably wasn't all that different, he was just going to have to keep doing what he'd been doing. But for some reason it was filed under a very different drawer in his mind.

When the credits rolled and the three of them headed out of the movie theater, Aurora quickened her step to fall in beside Michelle.

"Hey, I wanted to talk to you about something."

Michelle looked up expectantly, slipping her hand into Aurora's in the automatic way that she always did Dante's.

"I already talked to Dante about it," Aurora continued. "And he said I should ask you about it."

"Okay." Michelle looked back and forth between them. "You guys are getting married?"

"What? NO!"

Dante's ego took a healthy punch to the gut at Aurora's utterly horrified look. She turned and looked Dante straight in the face, practically begging for his help out of that particular conversation.

He raised his hands and his eyebrows at the same time. If she was so horrified at the prospect of marrying him then she could get herself out of this one.

"I… no. We're not getting married. That's not what I wanted to talk about."

"Okay," Michelle said, taking it on the chin. "Then what?"

"My company, Esposito Group, we throw fundraisers a few times a year for good causes. And this year I was thinking that we should do a fundraiser for research toward Von Willebrand's."

"Oh!" Michelle looked surprised as she pulled open the back door of Dante's car. "Really?"

"Yeah. I was thinking a lot about what you said about wishing that you knew more about the disorder. And we're always on the lookout for good causes."

"That's really cool, Aurora."

"So…" Aurora's gaze flicked to Dante for a half second as they slid into the front seats. "Will you make a speech?"

"What?!" Michelle screeched, her messy hair falling into her eyes. "Me?"

"I think everyone would really want to hear from someone who lives with the disorder. They'd want to know a little about what it is like to have it and what it would mean to you to know more about it." "I—I've never given a speech before."

"Come on, kid, you can do it," Dante jumped in. "You're made of words. Hell, you've never been speech-less before."

Aurora and Michelle grimaced at one another over Dante's bad joke, but Michelle instantly sobered. "Can I think about it?"

"Of course."

Dante knew when it was time to change the subject for Michelle. He knew when she chewed her lip, nervousness was rising in her belly. "You still wanting to go to that sleepover tonight?" he asked, half hoping that she'd say no.

"Yeah," she answered absently, still obviously

thinking over the idea of making a speech about Von Willebrand's in front of a bunch of adults.

"You don't have to go if you don't want to. I know I said it was a good idea before but—"

"No, no. You were right," Michelle agreed. "I like Teya. And she's never invited me to anything before, so I think I should probably go."

* * *

When they arrived home, Aurora wordlessly followed Michelle into her room and sat on the little girl's bed, making suggestions about what to pack. She could tell Michelle was a little nervous about her first sleepover with her new friend Teya. Dante had told Aurora that most of Michelle's friends were other kids from the hospital who were dealing with blood disorders. Which was cool, but she was just starting to make some public school friends as well.

Aurora was doing her best to stuff an oversized sleeping bag into an undersized backpack when Dante came back to the bedroom to find them.

"Time to go," he said.

"Mind if I wait for you here?" Aurora asked, one hand on her stomach. "I'm a little tired."

"You feeling alright?" Dante asked her, his eyes narrowing on the hand on her belly.

Aurora immediately dropped her hand. "Oh. Yes. Just a little tired is all."

Michelle held her hands out for a hug and Aurora wrapped her right up.

* * *

When Dante returned from dropping Michelle off at the sleepover, it was to find Aurora, heels kicked off, curled up on his living room couch.

He watched the soft rise and fall of her chest. Her hair was the messiest he'd ever seen it, the silky strands tangled over the throw pillow. She wore a casual green dress, a little boxy and made of t-shirt material. She'd been doing that more often lately, he'd noticed. Dressing casually on the weekends.

It made his mouth water. And it thrilled him. He felt like he was somehow bridging the gap between the two versions of her. The stiff and formal work version of her and the passionate, wild home version of her. On the weekends she was in the middle. Relaxed and casual and so stunning it almost hurt to look at her.

It was getting out of hand, he had to admit. His feelings for her. He'd thought that indulging in her would quench the thirst he felt for her. But if anything, it had increased it. The tastes he was getting never seemed as if they would be enough.

He didn't think she was necessarily using him to forget Gio anymore, but that didn't mean she still didn't have feelings for him. Even so, he sensed how things had changed between them. Just as Aurora was inside him, he'd found a place inside her. She enjoyed him in an elemental way, both in bed and out.

Unable to stand the distance between them a moment longer, he stepped closer to where she slept on the couch. As if she felt his eyes on her, she stirred, the long, golden column of her neck exposed against the early evening light.

Her eyes came open, blinking slowly, as if she were trying to figure out exactly who he was.

"Oh. Hi."

He cocked his head to one side, unable and unwilling to fight against the wave of tenderness that rose up inside him.

* * *

"I'm glad you're back," Aurora said as she struggled against the fatigue that weighed her down. Something about this stage of pregnancy had her dragging. She'd actually fallen asleep at her desk chair the other day. "There was something I wanted to talk to you about."

"You look cute all fuzzy from sleep."

"I'm sorry?"

"Normally you're gorgeous, flawless. But you've got lines from the pillow on your cheek, your eyes are all heavy, your hair's all messy and you just look cute."

Aurora raised an eyebrow, unsure whether to be insulted or charmed.

But she didn't have long to debate because seconds

later, Dante's hand snaked up her folded leg and just under the bottom hem of her dress.

Her breath caught in her chest.

He slid himself with the grace of an athlete on top of her, and she found herself absolutely drowning in a kiss. A kiss that bent all the rules of space and time for her. He was at once both comforting, calming, and deeply thrilling. Aurora was vaguely aware of the fact that she could barely feel her feet, that her hands had slid bonelessly from his cheeks. But she couldn't think much past the slow slide of his tongue against hers, of his teeth at her lip.

When the light changed, darkened and deepened, Dante rose with her in his arms. He carried her through the house and neither of them spoke. They'd kissed long enough that night had fallen without either of them turning on any lights and they didn't want to break the spell of it. They were warm and fuzzy and wrapped up in one another. The arousal that they'd just pulled from each other was a long, languid slide, devoid of the urgency that was so common in the way they usually touched one another.

When Dante laid her on the bed, stripped her clothes and then his own, Aurora said nothing. There were no words for it. When he speared his hands through her hair, took her lips in yet another waterfall of a kiss, Aurora said nothing. When his hand slid down the smooth plane of her back, over the curve of her ass, found her aching wetness, she said nothing. All she could do was feel and feel and feel.

But when he slid into her, she had to speak. There was one word that she simply had to say, like it was a spell that would keep the night from ever ending.

"Dante," she whispered into the dark, into the warm skin of his shoulder, her eyes squeezed tight and her hands in fists on his back. "Dante."

* * *

Dante froze before he reared back to catch her eyes with his. It was the first time she'd ever said his name during sex and it shook something loose inside of him. It was the first time he could be certain that she was thinking of him, and only him, while he was loving her body.

"Say it again," he demanded, his harsh voice a striking contrast to the tender way he held her.

"Dante."

The gentle, languid feelings that had been flowing through him heated, crystalized, sharpened. He found he didn't want to take her on a lazy river of passion. She'd said his name, stared into his eyes and now he wanted to eat her alive. His body demanded it.

Dante pulled out of her and Aurora gasped, moaning at the loss of him. He didn't make her wait long. Grasping her waist, Dante flipped her body around, and settled her on her hands and knees.

He took one necessary second to whisk a hand along her spine, smooth a palm over her glorious ass. But then he found he couldn't wait another moment. Dante lined himself up and plunged back into her.

Aurora moaned, her hips pushing back into him and grinding against his body like she couldn't get close enough.

Dante fell over her, his chest to her back, his hands on either sides of hers, his mouth at her ear.

"Say my name," he commanded as he rutted into her from behind.

She trembled with each of his punishing, delicious thrusts, her body scooting forward on the bed.

"Dante," she whispered on an endless moan.

Looking to the side he caught sight of them in the floor length mirror on the open door of his closet. He turned her head to look as well and she moaned and seized, her orgasm washing through her the second she caught sight of the animalistic scene.

His body, taut and lined, looming over hers, his muscles heavily shadowed in the moonlight. And her body, trembling, soft and taking everything he gave her.

Dante rutted her through her orgasm and on toward another. He dropped his head toward her ear and Aurora twisted her mouth to catch his.

"Dante," she whispered into his mouth.

It was enough to send both of them over the edge again. She was telling him that it was *him* who was fucking her, both in her body and in her mind. And as he exploded inside her, Dante realized that it was all he'd ever wanted.

* * *

"We have to get out of bed!" Aurora insisted the next morning. They'd been making out for damn near an hour. Dante was currently in the process of licking and sucking at that place on her neck he favored and she didn't think she could take another second.

He'd fully distracted her last night with all the sex and she was acutely aware of the major bomb she was about to drop on him. She just wanted it to be over.

Plus, she was starving and needed breakfast bad. Her stomach growled, loudly, to prove it.

Dante looked up at her, grinning. "You hungry, baby?"

"What do you think?" she asked, grinning right back and scooting to the edge of the bed.

She stretched, let her hair fall over her back and couldn't help but smile when she felt his fingers draw a picture on her back. It was like he couldn't go more than a few seconds without touching her.

"Plus," she said, looking over her shoulder at his sleepy face. "We've gotta make ourselves semi presentable for when Michelle gets back."

"She won't be back until this afternoon." Dante frowned and swung his legs out of bed. "I hope she's having fun. She said she'd call if she needed anything. But it's her first sleepover in a long time and…"

He trailed off, thoughtful. Aurora scooped one of his t-shirts from the dresser and carefully chose her words.

"For someone who draws such careful lines in the sand, you sure worry about her the way a father might."

Dante's eyes snapped up to her as he tugged on some boxers. "You know, lately, some of those lines are starting to get a little blurry for me. The line between brother and father."

"Oh?" Something tripped in Aurora's chest like a stone skipping across a lake.

"She told me the other day that she thinks of me like a dad. It shook me up."

"Why?" She followed him downstairs to the kitchen. He sat her up on the counter where he could look at her all he wanted and started to pull stuff out of the fridge to make them breakfast.

"Because I've always been so sure that I'll never be a dad. Because of my dad."

"He… is a bad guy?"

Dante seemed to weigh his words carefully. "Honestly, I don't know much about him as a person. But as a father? Well, yeah. He was a bad father. Neglectful, bored, annoyed. He treated me and my mother like we were the highest degree of burden. I would say that he withheld love, but honestly, I don't think he even had any love to withhold."

"Dante," Aurora whispered, horrified for what he must have gone through.

"I had no template for how to be loving or attentive." He pulled out some pans and poured her a cup of coffee. "So when Michelle first came to live with me, I found myself doing things my dad might do or say. And it horrified me. I realized that I was trying to be her father. And unfortunately, the only kind of father I can be is like my own dad. But when I changed the way I was thinking about it, called myself her brother instead, well, it gave me a chance to start from scratch. Have a new roadmap."

"That makes sense," Aurora said slowly. "But now…"

"Yeah. Now things are kind of changing. She's old enough that she understands what's going on. I've started realizing that it matters less how I think about it and matters more how she thinks about it. If she's thinking of me as her dad, then I guess in a lot of ways, I'm her dad."

His voice was deep and calm, but Aurora could hear the gravity of his words, how much it shook him to say the words out loud.

She swallowed coffee down her dry throat. "Does it make you think about having children of your own?"

Dante opened his mouth to answer just as his cellphone chirped on the counter beside him. He picked it up and answered.

"Hey squirt."

Aurora watched as Dante's eyes rounded and then quickly narrowed. "Okay. Sit tight. I'll be there in ten minutes. We're going to have to go to the hospital. Don't argue. And when you're completely fine and on your way home and we've averted a heart attack for me, then we're going to have a real long talk about what the hell you were doing jumping on a damn trampoline in the first place."

Aurora winced and jumped up immediately from the

counter. She hurried upstairs to grab his pants and shoes and shirt for him. The conversation they'd just had burned on the tip of her brain. She'd been so close then, so terribly close, to just telling him. But she swallowed the words back. He had Michelle to take care of now. And there was no way Aurora was getting in the way of that.

14

"You're sure you're both okay?" Aurora asked Dante two days later. It was probably the tenth time she'd asked the question, but the trip to the ER with Michelle had shaken her. It was the first time she'd witnessed not only Michelle bleeding—not overly much, but enough—and the first time she'd witnessed twin looks of fear on Michelle and Dante's faces when at first the doctors couldn't get the bleeding to stop. Despite the fear on Dante's face, however, he'd remained calm and reassuring, a stalwart presence for Michelle, hugging her or making her laugh as needed.

Thankfully, the doctors had finally stopped the bleeding and assured Dante that Michelle would be fine. After that, Aurora had kissed Michelle on the cheek and left, leaving them to get settled back at home without her interference. She'd kept in touch by phone and was already planning to head to Dante's house tonight to make them dinner.

"We're good, gorgeous. We'll be even better when we see you tonight."

"Me, too," she said. "I've missed you both."

The words came out naturally, and for a moment she didn't know why he was so silent on the other end of the line. As if she'd shocked him. As if he didn't know how to respond. But then he said, "We've missed you, too. So much I think you should come prepared to spend the night. What do you say?"

She didn't even hesitate. "I say yes. Maybe I'll even pick up a little something at the mall to model for you after Michelle goes to bed. Would you like that?"

"I like you, Aurora. Whatever you wear."

She sucked in a breath at his heartfelt words and had to suddenly blink back tears. Before she started sobbing, she said a hasty goodbye, hung up, then stared at the phone.

Tonight, she thought. Tonight I'm going to tell him.

And even though everything will change, nothing will change. Dante will want this baby. He'll want me. And together with Michelle, we'll be a family.

She was so certain of it that she practically walked on air for the next few hours. Remembering her promise to Dante, she ducked out at lunch to do some shopping. Thirty minutes later, she was in the dressing room. She already had some new lingerie picked out, and she'd decided to try on a gorgeous sky blue pencil dress, imagining the look on Dante's face when she wore it to the meeting he had with Esposito Group tomorrow.

Aurora sighed as she worked the sky blue dress up her hips and over her arms. To her surprise, she had to tug a little harder than usual to get the thing zipped and when she looked in the mirror...

She was showing. Not definitively. Not absolutely. But in this dress, in this lighting, she was no question pregnant.

Holy crap. She quickly unzipped the dress and surveyed her stomach while it was bare. Had Dante noticed? Obviously not, since he hadn't said anything. Maybe he'd noticed but been too polite to say anything, figuring she was just putting on a few pounds.

In just her bare skin she definitely had a small bump, but it could easily be confused for a food baby. She pulled the dress on again, zipped it right up. Once again, as far as what someone would conclude upon seeing her in this dress, there was no question. She was pregnant.

Aurora lowered herself down to the bench in the dressing room and placed her hand over her stomach. It was going to be okay. She'd decided to tell Dante anyway. And she could feel the little lima bean in there. She could feel the baby's life. The growing, gorgeous energy of it.

Tonight, she'd place Dante's hand on her belly. And he'd feel the baby's energy too. She just knew it.

She bought the dress. Wore it out of the store, in fact. She wasn't going to hide her pregnancy a second longer. She wasn't ashamed. She was proud. And she couldn't wait for Dante to know it.

Aurora tossed her things behind her desk when she

got back to the office and stepped over to her window. Dante wasn't far. In fact, if she craned her neck, she could almost see his office building down the street. Maybe she'd just walk over there and tell him. Why wait? Why—

"Aurora, do you have a second? I was wondering…" Gio stepped into her office but his words trailed right off as his eyes zeroed in on her belly in the blue dress. He shut her office door behind him. "Holy shit."

Aurora smiled a little, letting her eyes drop to her belly as well. Her palm found its way to the gentle curve. "You're telling me."

"I—uh didn't know." Gio cleared his throat. "I mean, of course I didn't know. You didn't tell me. I–uh—"

"It's okay, Gio." She was charmed at how the normally smooth Giovanni Esposito was absolutely tripping over his words. "I haven't told anybody really."

"Wow." Gio lowered himself down into the chair across from her desk. "You're going to be a mom."

"Yup," Aurora said, bobbing her head and coming around to lean on the desk in front of him.

Gio scrubbed his hand over his chin for a second. "Do you need any help? Is the father in the picture?"

His words warmed her heart and she remembered why she'd had feelings for him for so long. But as he sat there, handsome as hell and so kind, Aurora was also amazed at how intensely she'd misidentified her feelings for him. Sure, she'd had a crush. A good strong one. But love? No. Now that she knew what love was, she was confident she'd never felt it for the man in front of her.

"Yes, he's in the picture." Suddenly feeling nervous, she fiddled with the end of her braid. "Gio, I don't want to give you the wrong impression about me. But this pregnancy, it... wasn't planned."

"What do you mean 'the wrong impression'?"

"Well, our relationship, and my relationship to the company is one that's built on professionalism and I wouldn't want my actions to reflect—"

"Oh, fuck the company, Aurora. If some client is scandalized by working with an unwed mother then fuck them back to the 1950s. You think I care about any of that? I care about you! Your happiness. And the baby's."

Aurora's eyes filled. She hadn't realized how much she'd feared her colleagues discovering she was fallible and messy and passionate. All the things she'd tried so hard not to be for so long. All the things that Dante just pulled right out of her, like thread from a spool.

"I hope the father is as understanding as you are."

Gio rose then. "Is there a chance that he won't be?"

Aurora brushed at her tears. "No. Yes. I mean, he's very sweet. And even though he said he doesn't want children—" Right then her voice broke as emotion swept over her. She was ninety-nine percent sure that Dante would want her and the baby, but suddenly there was that teeny tiny percent that had her doubting everything they'd been to each other in the last few weeks. What if? What if she was wrong?

Before she knew what was happening, Gio cursed and drew her into his arms, her cheek pressed into his shoulder. Just months ago, she would have killed to hold Gio like this. Now, wrapped up in his arms, even as much as she appreciated his kindness, she wished he was Dante.

Dante. The father of her child. The man she loved.

* * *

Dante closed the door of Aurora's office as silently as he'd opened it. He allowed himself one second of leaning back against the wall. One second of searing pain in his chest. He had no breath and he was sure that his heart was skipping beats.

Hearing a noise from inside her office, he sprang forward, striding to the elevator and jamming the button. There was no way in hell he was going to let one of them come out of her office and catch him here in the lobby like the absolute tool he apparently was.

When the elevator didn't move fast enough, Dante slammed through the door for the stairwell, taking them four at a time on his way down. The image of Aurora's face as she'd clung to Gio was burned into his brain. He'd heard the sound of voices as he'd approached her door and opened it to find…that.

What the hell were they doing embracing in the middle of her office in the middle of the day?

Dante stopped walking and pressed a hand to her chest. Honestly, it didn't even matter what they'd been doing. It was how they'd been doing it that was so incriminating.

Aurora had her arms all the way around Gio. Her cheek pressed to his shoulder.

An expression of love on her face.

FUCK.

God. How could he have been such a fool? He'd truly thought things had changed between them. That even if she wasn't completely over Gio, she had equally strong feelings for Dante. Now he could see that had been all in his head. There was no way a woman could hold a man with that look on her face and not be in love.

Dante slammed out the back entrance of the building and immediately slid into the driver's seat of his car. He pulled his buzzing phone out of his pocket and read the text from Aurora with a mirthless laugh.

Are you free right now? There's something important I want to tell you and I don't want to wait.

Yeah, he just bet there was something she wanted to tell him. And god, it made him sick to his fucking stomach just to think about it. He could tell when a break up text was forthcoming. And he sure as hell wasn't going to sit there quietly while she explained about her feelings for another man. He was strong, but he had his limits.

Dante ignored the text, tossed his phone into the passenger seat and drove home.

15

Aurora frowned down at her phone. A small worm of worry had started to work its way through her brain. She'd texted Dante twice but hadn't heard back from him. Now the workday was over and she was supposed to meet him and Michelle at his place in about an hour. But damn it, she wanted to talk to him now. This time, however, she tried calling his office phone.

"Callaghan."

Her breath caught in her throat at the sound of his voice. Both because she loved him and his voice did stuff to her. But also because it appeared she'd been right to worry that he'd been ignoring her texts.

"Dante."

Several seconds ticked by before he clipped out, "Aurora."

She cleared her throat, suddenly grappling with the very strange sensation that she was speaking with a stranger. "Is everything alright? I tried reaching out a few times earlier today."

"Everything's fine. Same as it always was. Apparently."

What? She had no idea what that was supposed to mean. "Listen, do you have time to meet me now? I know we're supposed to meet at your place in a while but—"

"I know what you have to tell me. And I don't have time for it."

"I—what?" Aurora's heart stuttered in her chest. Her breath came out in a strangled puff. She couldn't have heard him correctly.

He knew she was pregnant? How?

"I came to your office earlier, Aurora. I saw you. I know."

Aurora's breath left her in a heavy rush and at the cold tone in his voice, she doubled over as if she'd been gut punched. One of her hands instinctively curled around her belly. "You saw?"

* * *

"You saw?"

At Aurora's guilty tone, Dante gritted his teeth. The image of her holding Gio so closely, so intensely, seared through Dante's brain for the five hundredth time. He'd trade five years off his life to have that memory scrubbed from his brain.

She was silent on the other end of the line now, obviously searching for something to say. He felt a sick sense of satisfaction over having stolen the words from her. He knew how calm and collected she was. How much thought she'd probably put into preparing what she was going to say to him. He was sure her little speech would have been gentle and respectful. And he wanted to hear it like he'd wanted a hole in his head.

He couldn't do it. Couldn't listen to her confess that she still loved Gio and they'd decided to be together. Couldn't do it and stay the same man that he was.

All that mattered was getting out of this shit ass situation alive. With his soul intact. And that meant severing things quickly and efficiently. It meant walking away from her before she could walk away from him. It meant being cruel.

Something clenched in Dante's gut. As mad as he was at her, as hurt as he was, he didn't want to treat her poorly. He loved her, goddamn it. Even now, with the image of her wrapped around another man, the man who truly had her heart, he still loved her. But he needed a clean break.

"Yes. I saw, and I can't do this with you. It's over. You know it. I know it."

* * *

Dante's words were poison in Aurora's ears but somehow she still managed to gasp out, "That's it? That's all you have to say?"

"I'm not sure what more you want me to say."

"You don't want us in your life at all?"

"I don't see how I could."

The silence between them stretched on. The idea of hanging up the phone and finalizing their separation was terrifying for Aurora, but what else could she do? Finally, she managed to take a deep breath and channel her inner strength.

She refused to permanently slam the door on her child's father. Her child deserved to have some hope of a future where he or she could know Dante. If she said something terrible, out of pain or anger, then she might close off that future forever. She wouldn't do that.

"If you change your mind, Dante, I'll never cut you out of our lives."

"Goodbye, Aurora."

She didn't say goodbye. She simply hung up the phone and stared, dimly, unseeing, into a future much more lonely than she had ever imagined for herself.

16

Two months later

Dante reclined in the lounger and watched Michelle splash around in the turquoise blue salt water pool on the deck of the resort. He wasn't drunk, because he was on vacation with Michelle, but he wished like hell that he could be.

He hadn't had a drink in two months and in some ways, it sucked to not have the dulled edges that alcohol provided. In other ways, he was glad to be seeing things so clearly. It kept him on his toes. Made him realize that he hadn't been wrong in the way he'd left things with Aurora.

The vacation he'd booked seconds after hanging up the phone with Aurora had turned into an extended sabbatical. He and Michelle had lit out for Spain and thank god it was summer break for her because he hadn't even been tempted to go back. Which didn't mean he hadn't replayed his last conversation with Aurora over and over again in his head. Looking for any way he could have done it differently. But if he'd given her more time, heard her out, it would simply have been a long, messy conversation, at the end of which he'd been wrecked. No way. He'd done the right thing in the long term. Quick and painful was better than long and painful.

"You coming in, Coco?" Michelle called, her feet dangling over the edge of an enormous floaty in the shape of a palm tree. The plus side of this forced vacation was that Dante and Michelle were closer than ever. He'd stopped correcting people who referred to her as his daughter. And Michelle either didn't notice or didn't mind.

He just hoped for once, Michelle wouldn't bring up Aurora anytime soon.

He'd made the mistake of being honest with her about the way they'd broken up. Michelle had been astonished and outraged.

"You left it just like that?!" she'd hollered at him, her hands on her hips, her hair a messy tumble. "There's so many ways you could have the wrong idea, Dante! You should have been more clear!"

But he wasn't budging. He wasn't letting Michelle change his mind about this. He knew what he'd seen.

He just wished he was getting over it a little faster. There were days, wandering through old Spanish villages with Michelle, or looking out at the ocean after she'd gone to sleep, that Dante thought he might finally be getting over Aurora. But then he'd find himself subconsciously reaching for her in the night and all of it would hit him like a hurricane.

He *wasn't* getting over her. He wished he could hate her for that. But no matter what he did, his stupid heart just kept loving her. It would be so much easier if he could be bitter and angry. But he couldn't stop himself from wishing her well.

Dante set his water bottle aside and did a running cannonball into the pool just to delight Michelle.

That night, they decided to wander into town, see if they could rustle up some seafood. Michelle walked next to him in a pair of jean shorts and shirt she'd picked out in Barcelona. It was surprisingly girly. Not her usual style. Red and flowy, the top had little dots and stars in a pinwheeling pattern.

Dante watched her walk for a second and realized, with a start, that she'd brushed her hair before they'd left the hotel. She was pushing eleven. Her birthday was in a month.

Soon she was going to be a teenager. Interested in dating and makeup and god knows what. The thought tightened his stomach. Dante had the impression that he was going to be spending a lot of time googling parenting techniques.

He thought of how natural Aurora had been with Michelle. How she'd helped Michelle pack her bags for the sleepover. How she'd stood beside them in the ER, comforting them both, lending her strength.

The thought was like a poisoned arrow in his heart. Aurora was never going to be that person for Michelle again. She was never going to be Dante's partner in raising her.

"Dante?" Michelle asked, dragging a fingertip from brick to brick of the old buildings they wove through.

"Yeah?"

"Would it be alright if I called Aurora?"

He came up short. It was almost like she'd read his mind. Why was she thinking about Aurora now?

Michelle glanced at him and quickly said, "I just didn't get to say goodbye. And I really liked her. And I just wanted to say goodbye."

Dante felt like the worst kind of jerk. Why hadn't he thought of that before? Michelle and Aurora had been close. Really close. Of course Michelle would want to talk to her again.

"I didn't mean to keep her from you. If you want to call her, you totally can. I'm sorry. I should have thought of that."

"It's okay," Michelle said as she craned her neck to watch some kids running down toward the beach. Then she glanced nervously up toward Dante. "That's, uh, not the only reason I want to talk to her again."

He raised an eyebrow at her and gestured for her to continue talking.

Michelle took a deep breath. "I want to tell her that I love her. That she felt more like family than just a friend."

Dante was quiet as they walked.

"Say something," she urged him.

"I'm not sure what to say, Michelle. I don't want to

tell you no, but I'm worried that you think it'll change something between Aurora and me. It won't. Things are really complicated and we can't be together. You know that."

"I know," Michelle said, reaching up for Dante's hand. "I don't want to tell her because I think it will change anything. I want to tell her because it's true. And not telling her feels like lying. And it feels bad. In here." She patted her chest and looked up at him. "You know what I mean?"

Dante scrubbed one of his hands over his newly trimmed hair. Just like that his genius baby sister had shined a light on something he'd been trying to keep in the dark for two months now. He and Aurora were over, but his feelings for her weren't. And he'd never told her how he felt. Not once. And as much as losing Aurora felt bad, he suspected what felt worse was knowing he'd taken the easy way out. He'd done it to protect himself. He'd figured ending things quickly, without hearing what she had to say or saying what he wanted to say, was the best. But two months later, he was still bleeding.

He'd let her walk away without expressing how he felt about her.

So maybe, just maybe, he needed to do something about that.

* * *

"Enough, Manman!" Aurora scowled as she pulled her

face clear of the makeup brush her mother was dragging over her eyelids. For some reason, Cedalie had been primping Aurora for over an hour for the Von Willebrand's fundraiser and it was annoying the heck out of her.

Maybe it was the late summer heat. Maybe it was the fact that she felt as big as a whale. Maybe it was that she was going stag to a fundraiser she'd planned to attend with Dante and Michelle. But her mother was about one more swipe of blush away from getting pushed into the ocean.

"I just want you to look perfect, child," Cedalie said for what had to be the hundredth time. Cedalie knew how hard the last two months had been for Aurora. She'd been a shell of herself for almost three weeks of it. Until one day, a light had kicked on. She'd told Cedalie that she wasn't wallowing anymore. She was following in her mother's footsteps. Raising a baby on her own, and doing it well, if not exactly fearlessly.

She still ached for Dante. And for Michelle. And for what could have been for her baby. But she had a life to live, one with her baby, and she was going to live that life and be the best mother she could be.

"Why do you even care, Mama? It's just a fundraiser. We have them three times a year and you've never cared before."

"I have a good feeling about tonight. I think you're going to get some romantic attention." Cedalie did up the last of the zipper on the midnight blue satin dress that cupped her breasts and swept over her very pregnant belly.

The dress had a long slit up one leg, the only feature on Aurora's body she didn't think looked whale-ish.

Aurora scoffed and started braiding her hair. "Romantic? Please. I look like I'm carrying triplets. No man is going to make a move on me tonight." And Dante is still halfway around the world in Spain, the last she'd heard. But she didn't add that part out loud.

"You never know," Cedalie said in a sing-song voice as she arranged a thin necklace of small amethyst crystals at Aurora's collarbone.

Aurora peeked out the window at the cab that had just pulled up. "Yeah. I know." She turned to go, felt guilty for snapping, and turned back. "But thank you for the effort."

Cedalie kissed her daughter's cheek, laid a hand over her grandchild, and gently pushed Aurora out the door.

Aurora tried not to groan as they pulled up to the hotel where the fundraiser was being hosted. She knew that Gio and Rose were going to be inside, which, in a strange turn of events, was actually a comfort to her. When it had become very clear that the father of her child had not taken the news well, both Gio and Rose had reached out to her many times. She often found herself with some leftovers at lunch, chatting with Rose and Gio in one of their offices.

She'd never in a million years have thought that would be the case and she cherished her new friendships.

She arranged her dress, smoothing it down, and stepped into the grand ballroom. The space had been transformed with glittery decorations and rows and rows of items they'd gathered for the silent auction part of the fundraiser. The culminating event at the end would be a live auction, and one of the most generous items had been given by Gio himself—a year of his consulting services.

She wandered through the event space, tidying this and that and greeting the first guests who arrived. She couldn't help the dull ache in her heart whenever she thought of Michelle. She'd put the whole thing together as a way of encouraging the little girl. Wanting to give her hope for a brighter future.

Aurora sighed. She'd really hoped to share the evening with her. But according to Gio, who still didn't know that Dante was the father, he and Michelle had left town for an extended summer vacation over two months before. They were hopping from villa to villa in Spain.

Aurora had found herself insanely jealous of Spain for getting to be with them.

Ugh. She was so sick of being sad. Not for the first time, Aurora hoped that these kinds of feelings weren't affecting the baby. Because if so, she was going to be raising one melancholy kid.

Minutes later, the band kicked on. The party started full swing, and Aurora pasted on the best smile she could muster up.

* * *

Dante was cranky, tired, starving, and thirsty. He'd been on four planes, a train, and two taxis in the last 24 hours. After two months of sandals and shorts, his tux felt like a prison jumpsuit, and it seemed like every person he ran into wanted to say five hundred things he couldn't care less about.

When he and Michelle had gotten off the plane, the first thing Dante had done was call Aurora. But it had been Cedalie who'd answered the phone.

"You're a stubborn one, Dante Callaghan," she'd said.

Dante had raised his eyes to the sky, pinched the bridge of his nose, and then wondered idly if Cedalie was enough of a psychic to know that he'd done just that. "I really need to talk to her, Cedalie."

"Yes, you do."

"Can you put her on?" He attempted to summon patience from some deep, deep well that he sincerely hoped he had.

"She left her phone behind tonight by accident. But you could meet her at the gala, which you will, if you're feeling impatient, which you are."

"Right. What gala?"

"The Von Willebrand's fundraiser that she's been planning? Over at the Hilton Ballroom."

Dante had felt as if he'd been punched in the face. Of course she'd still gone through with planning that fundraiser. Because she was such a good person with such a good heart.

"Right," he'd said again. And hung up.

He'd stopped home long enough to grab a dress for Michelle and a tux for himself.

And now he was wading through the rich clientele of

this fundraiser and desperately searching for Aurora. Michelle had floated over toward the buffet table the minute they'd come in, and that was fine by him. He'd rather not have an audience for the emotional ransacking he was sure he was in for.

Dante scanned the crowd yet again. Even though he didn't see Aurora, however, something else caught his eye.

Giovanni Esposito pulling a little redheaded woman into a back hallway, crowding her up against a wall.

What. The. Fuck.

Dante saw red. Gio was still fucking around with Rose when he and Aurora were together? Or, even worse, had Aurora agreed to be his side piece?

Dante bowled through the crowd, not giving a royal fuck whose champagne he was spilling as he made a straight line for Gio.

Rose ducked through the bathroom door just as Dante rounded the corner of the hall. He found himself face-to-face with a smugly grinning Gio.

Dante cold cocked Gio right in his dumb, handsome face.

"Jesus fucking lord, Dante!" Gio doubled over, checked his lip for blood, and straightened. "What the hell is wrong with you?"

Dante was vibrating with barely contained rage. "I cannot fucking believe you'd do that to Aurora." He viciously pointed toward the door Rose had just walked through.

Gio looked behind him, seemingly completely

confused. "What?"

"You're out here, publicly messing around with Rose right in Aurora's face? Can't you see that she's a person? She's the best fucking person? She's got a heart the size of the universe and she seems so calm and cool, like she can handle anything, but she's fragile too. And you can't just treat her like this. Like she's disposable." Dante had Gio backed against the wall of the hallway, each word wrenching out of him like a knife.

"Yeah, I know everything you're saying, asshole. But I still don't know what kissing my wife at a party has to do with Aurora." Gio shoved Dante backward. "Or what it has to do with your dumb ass."

Dante blinked at Gio. "You're actually trying to pretend you're not hooking up with Aurora on the side? Stringing her along?"

Gio's mouth fell dead open. "What. The. Fuck."

Dante's brow furrowed. That reaction had seemed genuinely shocked.

"I have never, nor will I ever, hook up with Aurora LeMonde. She's my good friend and business partner. And I love my wife, you son of a bitch."

Dante stepped back. Confused and irritated. "But I saw you."

"You saw me what?"

Suddenly Dante's evidence seemed very small. Irritatingly small. "I saw you hugging her in her office a few months ago. It looked like you were…"

He trailed off.

Gio squinted his eyes, looking for all the world as if he was wracking his brain. "Hugging Aurora in her office? I have no idea what you're... *Oh*. That was the day I found out about her pregnancy. I was consoling her because she didn't know how the father was going to react to the news."

If Gio said more, if the world kept spinning, Dante had absolutely no awareness of it. He was stunned. Utterly and completely stunned.

The last few months replayed in his head in both slow and fast motion. He felt as if his life were a spinning top that someone had just flicked to the side.

Gio, reading Dante's face, took a step back, a little stunned himself. "You?"

Gio took a step forward then, instantly furious on Aurora's behalf. "You're the asshole that left her without so much as a good luck?"

Dante scraped a hand over his face, wishing that his blood would start pumping again so that he could just *think*.

"Was she showing?"

"What?"

"That day in her office, was she showing? If I'd walked in and you hadn't been blocking her belly, would I have known she was pregnant?"

"Yes, that's how I found out in the first place."

"Oh god. I didn't see. I didn't know." Dante crouched down and dragged his hands through his hair. He needed air. He looked up at Gio in absolute horror at what he'd done. "She said 'us'. She said 'our lives'."

"What?"

"I thought you two were together. That she was leaving me for you. She said 'us' and I thought she meant you two. But she meant her and the baby. She thought I knew she was pregnant and was throwing her away. FUCK."

Gio, reached down and dragged Dante back to standing. "Okay man, that's really bad. Jesus, really bad. But you've gotta find her and explain. Step one. Just explain. Okay?"

Dante was already tearing away from his hands and jogging back into the party. His eyes wild and his heart racing.

When he spotted her standing in the corner of the ballroom, sipping from a glass of ice water and politely nodding her head at something George Mills Junior was saying to her, Dante literally stopped in his tracks.

First it was her face that stopped him. Her precious, gorgeous face, all sharp lines and big eyes. Pregnancy had made her just a bit softer, but no less beautiful. And then his eyes travelled down. To the swell of her breasts. And further down, to her rounded belly. Full with child. His child.

Dante couldn't breathe. He wished he could say it was because of how beautiful she was, how happy he was to take this next step with her. But there was a healthy dose of raw fear in there as well. A kid. His kid. Holy shit. Dante sidestepped to the bar, signaled for a glass of whiskey, took a quick slug. He glanced around the room, clocked Michelle talking with Rose over by the buffet, then set his sights back on Aurora.

He steeled himself. Nothing left to do but nut up and go talk to her.

* * *

"So I told him that's a firm 'no'. If he wants to mess around with my money then I'm just going to take it elsewhere," George Junior said, snorting into his drink in a move he'd seen his father execute many a time. It didn't quite have the same effect.

Aurora did her best not to yawn but she wasn't sure she could handle another word from George Junior without passing out from boredom. The man was obviously trying his best to impress her with his newfound business acumen. He'd started the conversation with his eyes glued to her belly. From there, he'd talked nonstop about how responsible, competent, and reliable he was. Aurora was vaguely touched that George Junior was still interested in her, even with the baby on board. But she was also ridiculously annoyed that the 'romance' her mother implied she had in store for herself tonight was currently staring down the front of her dress.

Aurora pointedly cleared her throat and George Junior blushed, right down to the shiny bald patch at the crown of his head.

He took a deep breath. "You know, Aurora, I'm a

very rich man."

She raised an eyebrow.

"I could make it so you'd never have to work again," he plowed on.

Aurora shifted on her feet, which were really starting to kill her. She thanked god that Gio was starting to jog toward the stage. The second he auctioned off his consulting services, the night would pretty much be over and she could get the hell out of here and face-plant into her bed. No wait, she thought, looking down at her large belly... She could side-plant onto her bed. Then George Junior's words filtered up to her. This guy was a real class act. Not.

"Are you offering to pay me for my services, Mr. Mills?"

George Junior opened and closed his mouth like a fish out of water. "Not exactly. I'm just saying that if we were to be... close, then you'd have access to certain resources."

Bile rose in Aurora's throat as she took a decisive step backward. Smack into a solid, warm wall that pressed one hand against her lower back in the most familiar, delicious way. Her heart stopped.

"How many times am I going to have to tell you to quit while you're ahead, Junior?" Dante's voice washed over her.

George Junior's eyes narrowed. "Callaghan. I thought you skipped town. Left all your business deals in the breeze?"

Aurora willed her heart to start beating. She willed herself to turn and make sure he was truly there. But nothing happened. Her body was completely frozen in place.

"Well, I'm back now. And I'd appreciate it if you'd stop looking down Ms. LeMonde's dress."

George Junior balled his hands up and jammed them in the pocket of his suit. "You're such a fucking prick, Callaghan. And you just lost yourself a valuable client." He turned and stomped into the crowd.

"For all his sudden interest in his father's business, he doesn't even realize that he was never your client in the first place," Aurora mused, her brain latching on to any detail that she could right now. Because suddenly Dante was there, in front of her. Deep blue eyes and short hair. He was a toasty tan with a short, full beard. God, he looked good enough to swallow whole.

But his eyes were pained, horrified, desperate.

He stood in front of her, gripping her shoulders. "Aurora—"

"You came back." She felt as if she were in a dream, her words floating out of her and toward him on a lazy river.

"Yes. Michelle and I came back. I have to talk to you right now. Can we go outside?"

Aurora took a deep breath. Her vision blurred everything but his face, which was in bright, sharp definition, almost painful to look at. He wanted to talk with her. He had things to say. After two months of complete silence, the thought of actually having a conversation with him was like starving for weeks and then sitting down to a plate of filet mignon.

She'd have settled for a text.

But here he was, in full living color.

"Dante," she started, lifting a hand to her hair in a lost, absent gesture. "I—"

"Aurora, will you join me on stage?" Gio's voice carried through the banquet hall. She was dimly aware that he'd been speaking to the crowd through the microphone, explaining about Von Willebrand's and thanking people for their generous donations. He must be about to auction off the consulting services. Is that why he needed her onstage?

Dazed, as if she were wading through hip deep water, Aurora stepped away from Dante and toward Gio onstage.

* * *

She was walking away. Dante's breath came fast. She was walking away from him. But not before she'd looked at him like he was the fucking Ghost of Christmas Past. Stunned. Wrecked. He'd never seen Aurora look that caught off guard. And he didn't blame her. Her baby daddy shows up out of nowhere and she's supposed to what? Leap for joy?

He watched as Gio helped her up onstage. Dante glanced down at Michelle pulling on his pocket.

"What happened? Did you tell her? Did you know she

was pregnant?"

Dante scrubbed a hand over his face. "I had no idea she was pregnant and no I didn't tell her I love her yet."

Then, with surprising strength for a ten-year-old girl, Michelle reached up and tugged his face down toward hers. "I swear to god, Coco. The first chance you get, you tell her everything. All of it. And you better be crystal fucking clear."

Dante blinked at her, straightened up and stared at Aurora, so gorgeous she made his heart contract. "Got it."

He glanced back down at Michelle. "And we'll talk about your use of the F-word later."

"Yeah, yeah." She waved a hand through the air. "You can ground me later."

Dante cocked an ear, listened to what Gio was saying.

"Not only has Ms. LeMonde planned this entire event, but the final item up for auction tonight is actually Ms. LeMonde herself." Whispers and cheers broke out in the crowd as Aurora went sheet white on stage. She tugged Gio's shoulder, furiously whispering in his ear.

Dante's head started to buzz.

Gio patted Aurora's shoulder and continued to talk into the microphone. "Esposito Group would like to put up for auction one year of Ms. LeMonde's consulting services. And as her friend and business partner, I can tell you that there is no one smarter, sharper, or more hard working." He pushed Aurora slightly forward.

Dante could see how much she was currently wishing she could be anywhere else. And then he saw her professionalism kick in. Her smooth and polished exterior immediately covered up her insecurities. One hand automatically rested over her rounded belly.

Her child. His child. Their child.

"Let's start the bidding at $5,000," Gio's voice echoed out through the room.

* * *

Aurora inwardly groaned as George Junior's pink hand raised at one end of the room. Oh lord. It was that perv's dream come true. He could actually use his money to purchase her.

"One hundred thousand dollars," said a deep, familiar voice.

Aurora didn't have anything in her mouth to choke on but air, but choke she did. Dante waded through the sea of murmuring, whispering people. His eyes burned into hers like hot coals. She was pinned in place, her mouth dropped right open.

"Yes. Well. That'll do it, I think. Thank you to Mr. Callaghan, and please, enjoy the rest of the evening." Gio, grinning like a Cheshire cat, flipped the microphone off right as Dante bounded up onto the stage.

"Dante, you can't— Are you crazy? That's too much!"

"Aurora," Dante said as he grabbed her ice-cold hands. "I have the fucking money, it's going towards research for the disorder my sister has, and it gets you off the goddamn auction block. You're insane if you think you can talk me out of this."

With that, he swept one arm under her knees and lifted her up like she hadn't gained twenty pounds in the last two months.

Dante turned to Gio, who was still grinning. "And don't think I don't realize what you did, auctioning her services instead of yours."

Gio shrugged and gestured to his swelling lip. "We're even now."

Dante grunted and strode off the stage behind the velvet purple curtains at the back. He set Aurora down on a folding chair and immediately fell to his knees in front of her. The bright lights of the ballroom filtered through the cracks in the curtains and painted patterns across both their faces.

"I've got shit to say and Michelle says I need to be crystal fucking clear so just don't talk and let me say it all, okay?"

Aurora, her heart still racing, merely nodded.

"I didn't know you were pregnant until ten minutes ago."

Aurora's brow furrowed, her mouth dropped open and she drew breath to say something. Dante simply clapped a hand over her mouth and bit back the heat that seared through him at the feel of her lips on his palm.

"That day, the thing that I saw? It was you hugging Gio. I opened the door to your office and saw you pressed up against him. I—I knew that you loved him, that you were using me to get him out of your system, and for a while that was alright with me but..."

He stood and began pacing in front of her.

"But seeing the two of you like that... the love all over your face, love that I wanted for myself, it almost destroyed me. So I ended things. I ended things fast. And I did it without telling you how I feel about you."

He dropped to his knees in front of her again. "It killed me, Aurora. You said 'us', you said 'our lives', on that phone call, and I thought you were talking about you and Gio as a couple. But earlier, after I got here, I confronted Gio. He said you were already showing that day, but I didn't see your belly. I didn't know."

"If you didn't know, then why are you here?"

He cupped her face in both his hands. "Because I'm in love with you. So goddamn in love with you. So much that even though I knew that you were with Gio, the love of *your* life, I still had to tell you. I couldn't go on without telling you. And then I walk in here, run into Gio, and he just drops the bomb. You're pregnant. And I know it's mine. Maybe it's your witchy mother rubbing off on me, but I can look at you right now and I can *feel* that baby in there. That baby is mine. But I wouldn't care if the baby was Gio's. I wouldn't care if the baby was George Junior's. I love you, Aurora. I love you so much. I want both of you. You and the baby."

Aurora sat perfectly still. He watched as the professional veneer melted away under the heat of her passionate side. He watched in fascination and relief as she rose to stand in front of him, temper sparking over her face.

"You're saying that you want to be a part of the baby's life? Just like that? You're suddenly ready to be a father?"

"No, not just like that." He rose too, his temper making him pace again. "It's been four years of having Michelle. Of slowly getting used to the idea of being a parent. It took losing you and realizing that if I had to, I *could* live without you. Because of Michelle. Brokenhearted or not, I'd have to find a way to go on, even though I'd never be whole again. And, I don't know, but I think that makes me a father. And I'll make mistakes, Aurora. I know I will. But I'll be there." He stepped toward her. "Please, let me be there."

She stared at him, energy crackling between them. "I would never keep you from the baby, Dante. Even when I thought you were leaving me because I was pregnant, I couldn't do that. Don't you remember the last thing I said?"

"That you would never cut me out of your lives."

She nodded. "If it's the baby you want, we'll figure it out. We'll make it work together."

"I want the baby. And no matter what, that's never going to change. But Aurora, I need to be very, very clear here. I want you too. You love Michelle, I could see that from the beginning. So that won't be a problem. And you enjoy me. I'll do everything I can to make that enough. Even if you always love Gio, I'll try to make you happy—

"

Aurora burst out a small, hysterical laugh and slammed a hand over his mouth. "Enough." She took Dante by the shoulders and shook him hard. "I was thinking of you, you dumbass."

"What?" he asked.

"That day in my office, Gio asked me if the father would understand about the baby. I was hugging *him* but I was thinking of you. Thinking how badly I hoped you'd still want me after you found out I was pregnant."

Dante's mouth opened and closed. His brow furrowed.

Aurora plowed on. "I'm six months along, Dante. Which means—"

"I got you pregnant that first night. After the gala."

"Probably across the hood of your car." She lifted a wry eyebrow. "I wasn't thinking of Gio when I was with you that night. You filled my every thought. And afterward, I was still sad about Gio, lonely and rejected. But I couldn't stop thinking about you. Especially with all those damn flowers."

He smiled.

"And then I found out I was pregnant. I was horny as hell and confused and sad and I wanted you so badly. And there you were, offering yourself up, no strings attached, and I took my chance." She took a deep breath and let one of her thumbs trace a small circle over the pulse point at his neck. "I started sleeping with you. But it was never for the reasons you thought."

"You weren't using me to get over Gio?"

She shook her head. "Honestly, I don't think I thought of Gio again after that night in your entryway."

A sun rose in Dante's chest but he beat it back. He needed to know the rest. "You weren't thinking of him when I touched you?"

Now Aurora threw her head back and laughed, really laughed. Dante wasn't quite sure how to feel about that. He was halfway between scowling and laughing himself.

"Dante, I told you once and I'll tell you again. You suck all the oxygen out of the room for me. You're so undeniably you. There absolutely is no pretending it's not you." She traced her hand over his lips, his nose. "Your scent, your voice, your presence, it calls to me, Dante. It was only you for me. And when I realized I loved you... I should have told you sooner. About my love and about the baby. And I'm so sorry now I didn't. But I'm not sorry you're here. And I'm not sorry we have a second chance."

Dante hadn't realized the shadow that had still been hovering over him, not until he felt it lift. Not until he felt the sun rise. He felt it explode through him. Kneeling before her again, Dante let his forehead fall forward and rest on her rounded belly. And he felt something real, something electric and strong, zip through him.

He raised his head in surprise and blinked at Aurora.

"You felt it too?" she asked, swiping a hand over her belly.

He nodded and carefully placed his hand over hers.

He felt it again. A swell of energy so strong it raised

the hairs on his arm.

"What is it?" he asked.

"Love."

Dante rose. "So let me get this straight. I love you. And you love me."

"Yup."

"And we're having a baby."

"Yup."

"And you're going to date the hell out of me while we figure this shit out."

Aurora's eyes widened and filled with tears. He swiped at them as they rolled over her rounded, golden cheeks. Then he leaned forward and pressed his lips to hers. Her plush mouth melted against his and he felt the zing he always did when she was near. The heat and the warmth.

The fire that was Aurora.

She pulled away, blinked the tears out of her eyes, and took a deep breath. "Yup."

EPILOGUE

One year later

Aurora peeked out the kitchen window toward the back deck as she washed some tomatoes under the spray of the sink. She smiled at the sight there.

Michelle listened very carefully as Cedalie, sitting on the deck stairs just below her, held up a tarot card. Needless to say, Michelle and Cedalie got along very well. In her lap, Michelle cradled her baby brother, Dante "Cal" Callaghan Jr., Aurora's sweet little boy with his daddy's blue eyes.

Aurora had moved into Dante's house about two seconds after the auction. Every second since, Dante had taken care of her and their baby. After Cal was born, he did just as many midnight wake-ups as she did. He delighted in Cal's every spit bubble just as much as she did. And god only knew, he loved that baby just as much as she did.

Aurora shook her head, amazed at how lucky she was.

"You spying on them?" Dante asked as he came up behind her and wrapped his arms around her waist. He peeked through the window as well, chuckling when Cedalie drew another tarot card. "If we're not careful, we're going to have two fortune tellers on our hands."

"Three," Aurora corrected. "Have you seen how Cal looks at my mother when she talks?"

"Oh lord." Dante groaned. "I'll be outnumbered."

"You love it."

"Yes," he murmured against the soft skin of her neck. "I do."

Aurora let his love wash through her. "Dante," she said, turning in his arms, loving the way he pressed her up against the sink.

"Hmmm?" He nuzzled the skin just below her ear.

"I don't want to date you anymore."

He stiffened.

"I wanna be married to you."

His head popped up and his eyes burned into hers, utter shock in every line of his face.

"Will you marry me?" she asked.

Dante's eyes widened before he stepped away from her and let out a shaky laugh.

"You really know how to take the wind out of a guy's sails, gorgeous."

"What?"

He stalked to the drawer below the silverware and took out a small, black box, which he held up. "I was going to ask you this weekend, but since you're so antsy to get the show on the road, I guess you can have this a few days early."

Walking back to her, he gently placed the box in the palm of her hand. When Aurora opened it, she grinned at the small crystals set so perfectly in a gold setting.

"Your mother helped me pick the right gems. That one's for patience, that one's for emotional well being, that one's for passion, and that one's for creativity. They're all good magic, she says."

Aurora set the box on the counter and kissed the daylights out of him. "I'm taking the fact that you endured gem shopping with my mother as an indication you're saying yes to my proposal?"

"It's my proposal," he corrected. "Are *you* saying yes?"

She grinned. "Let's go ahead and both say yes."

He kissed her gently. "Then yes, my love. Yes, to marrying you. Yes, to living the rest of our lives together. Yes, yes, yes."

"Yes," she echoed, and twenty minutes later, in their bed, content in the knowledge that their children were safe with her mother, Aurora kept saying yes even as she dreamed of the day she'd soon stand in front of the entire world and say the words "I do."

**Thank you for reading
Bedding The Baby Daddy.**

If you enjoyed spending time with these characters,
be sure to check out Gio and Rose's story in Book 10!

Also, be sure to check out my sports romance series,
Going Deep. Here's a sneak peek of Book 1, **Down Deep**:

Excerpt
DOWN DEEP

PROLOGUE

Football players possess the ideal combination of strength and endurance.

And the best asses of any other athletes.

At least, that's what Sheila, Camille Pollert's best friend, once said. Sheila's cousin Mindy had thought Sheila was crazy. She'd claimed no one could beat soccer players for sheer sexiness.

But with her gaze focused squarely on #24's ass, Camille was definitely calling the play in Sheila's favor.

Of course, since Camille had been in love with the boy currently wearing the #24 jersey since freshman year, she supposed she was a bit biased.

Football players grunted and tackled each other, and the shrill sound of a whistle filled the air. She quickly took a few photos before wandering around the outskirts of the field. Always looking for the perfect shot, she hardly even noticed the screams and shouts of the students in the bleachers or the off-key blaring of the marching band.

A senior in high school, she had been part of the yearbook staff since ninth grade, but this was her first big assignment. But she wasn't *just* taking photos for the yearbook. Some of the photos she was taking for herself, to hide away in her box of photos documenting her crush on the most popular boy in school: Heath Dawson, player #24.

Camille heard one of the coaches yell something at the ref, and the ref warned him to back off. He didn't. She walked over to the long bench where some of the home team was sitting, all of them watching the ref and coach argue. She took a photo, liking how the shot radiated the edginess that she could feel coming off the team in waves.

Finally, the ref made an offside call against the visiting team and instituted a five-yard penalty. The players on the bench cheered while those on the field began to huddle up for the next play. Camille stayed at the bench, snapping photos.

At one point, Heath jumped into the air to catch the ball. Turning upfield and toward the end zone, he weaved agilely around the cornerback. Out of nowhere, the free safety came in, lowered his shoulder pads, and hit Heath square in the chest, causing the ball to fall.

The defensive cornerback scrambled and fell on the ball, recovering it for the defense.

The angry screech of the whistle sounded.

Camille held her breath as Heath lay on the ground, unmoving, but then finally, he shook himself off and stood. Looking both angry and crestfallen, he jogged back to the sidelines.

She blushed, her heart picking up speed when she realized he was headed right toward her where she stood by the water table. He was still several feet away when he took off his helmet. He shook his head, his sweaty dark locks brushing across his forehead, and he smiled gamely when a teammate slapped him on the shoulder. But his expression grew cloudier when he glanced up into the stands at an older man—Camille had seen them together enough to know it was his father—glowering, yelling something that she couldn't catch.

Heath walked right by her without even noticing her, which unfortunately wasn't anything new.

Even though Camille's father had coached Heath when he was just starting to play football, she'd never actually met him until ninth grade. That day, however, was forever burned into her memory. Their lockers had been next to each other, and when she'd been trying to reach up and place her books on the top shelf, Heath had stepped in and helped her. "Having trouble there?" he'd asked with a grin. His hand had brushed hers, and she had jumped away with a bright blush. He had looked her up and down, as if trying to place her, but when she was too tongue-tied to say anything, he had shrugged and turned back to his conversation with one of his buddies.

Heath smiling at her and helping her had made her heart beat so fast she was surprised she hadn't passed out. Not many girls got to be so close to him, and her appreciation for his help quickly blossomed into a fully-fledged crush. She snapped photos of him around school, she dreamed of him asking her out and telling her he loved her, and she blushed every time she heard his loud laugh in the hallways. As locker buddies, she had the opportunity to see him almost every day, although she never had the courage to talk to him. Just being close to him had been enough for her.

Sadly, the next year they were no longer locker buddies, but she'd always looked for him. She'd wanted to see his smile and hear his laugh, even if he didn't know she existed.

She was so preoccupied thinking about her history with Heath that she hadn't realized he was standing right next to her until he shoved a water cup into her hand. "Dude, refill this for me?" he asked, his gaze on the field.

Camille stared at the cup, nonplussed, before stammering, "I'm not the waterboy." She thrust the cup back in Heath's direction.

His gaze jerked to her face, and for a moment, he looked embarrassed before he grinned. "My bad. You're definitely *not* a waterboy."

Amused more than insulted, Camille glanced down at herself—jeans and an oversized football jersey with stained tennis shoes—and she shrugged. "I can see how you'd think that." She refused to apologize for being a tomboy or for how she dressed.

Heath squinted at her. "No, it's not the clothes. It's the hair. It's too short. You should think about growing it out." He returned his glance to the field, waving at a teammate before glancing back at her. "Have we met? What's your name?"

Not surprised he hadn't recognized her as his silent locker buddy from ninth grade, she fingered her hair. She had always worn it short—at the moment it was about chin-length— because she didn't know a lot about hair or make-up. Her mother had died when she was five, and her single father wasn't exactly into fashion. Plus Camille's naturally wavy hair could be so temperamental. But maybe Heath was right. Maybe she looked too much like a boy with short hair like this. Then she bristled, annoyed with herself for even considering his suggestion. What right did he have to give her style advice? When he looked at her again, though, an eyebrow raised, she blushed and stuttered, "I'm Camille."

"Well, Camille, you should eat something, girl." Looking her up and down, Heath added, "You're too skinny. You'd look great with some curves." His gaze landed on her breasts—or lack thereof—and Camille crossed her arms over her chest. She knew she was flat-chested and scrawny and didn't look like the kinds of girls Heath dated—curvaceous and blond and tan—but she couldn't believe he was being such an ass.

He had no right to talk to her like that. He didn't even know her! What kind of guy told a girl she needed to eat more because she was too skinny? Camille ate as much as any person.

Heath was still watching her, and a frown had overcome his expression.

Camille wasn't quick to anger, but when she was truly pissed, her friends and family knew there'd be hell to pay. She opened her mouth to tell him to go to hell when a harsh voice barked something from behind her, making them both jump.

"Would you stop talking to the waterboy and concentrate for once?" a man yelled.

Camille spun around, and saw Heath's dad stalking toward them. He looked so incensed she immediately took a step back, bumping into Heath.

He put a hand on her shoulder and gently moved her behind him, as if he was actually trying to protect her from his father.

"What the hell was that out there?" Heath's dad ranted. "When are you going to get it into your thick skull that without a scholarship, you aren't going anywhere?"

Heath glanced back at her, concern and something

darker overtaking the frown on his face. While part of Camille wanted to rush to his defense and tell his hateful father that Heath was the best wide-receiver in the state, she was too humiliated given Heath's father, just like his son, had mistaken her for a boy.

She clutched her camera close to her body, like a shield. Heath said something she didn't catch, and his dad replied, "You're a *girl?*"

It was too much. She skittered off the field and even though she thought she heard someone call her name, she didn't stop. She hid out under the bleachers for the remainder of the quarter, glad that no one bothered her as tears poured down her face. She felt silly for being so hurt by what Heath and his dad had said, but sometimes the barbs about her appearance became too much.

After the tears had dried up, anger took the place of her humiliation. Hatred for Heath completely eclipsed any kinder feelings she'd had toward him, and her crush on him disintegrated almost as quickly as it had started. So what if he'd helped her that one time and smiled at her? So what if he was the cutest boy in school and made her heart pound? She had no interest in being in love with a guy who was such a jerk, and if she'd known he was that awful, she'd never have fallen for him in the first place. He'd been the star football player, unattainable and handsome and popular, and she had idolized him from the moment she'd first seen him.

Now, though, she wanted to go straight home and tear up her journals where she'd doodled his name and hers in hearts across pages and pages of notebook paper. She wanted to burn the MASH game where it was predicted that she'd marry Heath and have 100 children and live in a mansion with him. And the photos she'd taken of him around school would go in the trash, too. All of it. She was done with Heath Dawson.

"Hey, what're you doing down here?" Camille turned to see her best friend Sheila climbing in next to her, her bright red hair unmistakable. "I thought you had to take pictures tonight?"

Camille wiped her face of any tearstains, hoping Sheila wouldn't see she'd been crying. "I was. I did. I'm taking a break."

"Underneath the bleachers, below the marching band?" Sheila glanced up as one of the drummers dropped a stick and swore.

"It's as good a place as any."

"Uh huh. I'm supposed to believe you're taking a break in the final quarter when you'd been wanting this assignment since you joined yearbook?"

Camille glared at Sheila, but her friend just smiled. Sighing, Camille rolled her eyes. "Fine. I'm hiding out. Happy?"

"Not until you spill the details of who, what, when, where, why, and to what extent."

"Heath Dawson is a jackass."

Sheila's eyebrows rose until they disappeared below her bangs. "Did he say something to you?"

Camille really didn't want to have this conversation,

but she also knew Sheila wouldn't leave well enough alone otherwise. Caving, she recounted what Heath and his dad said about her, feeling the hot press of anger in her chest once again when thinking about it. "Who says stuff like that?" she asked in a huff.

"Jackasses like Heath Dawson, for one. And quadruple jackasses like his father. The guy's so hard on his son, I almost feel sorry for him. But I always told you Heath wasn't worth your time. Would you listen to me? Noooooooo." Sheila gestured toward Camille. "And now look at you. Heartbroken, discarded, a shell of your former self."

Camille pushed her friend lightly, smiling for the first time. "You're stupid. And I'm not going to let this destroy me. He's not worth it."

"Atta girl! So, did you get some good shots?"

Camille picked up her camera and began going through the photos, seeing if she had enough to give to Trevor tomorrow in yearbook or if she needed to get back out there and take some more. Most of the shots were mediocre, although Camille found a handful that were definitely nice enough to be featured in the yearbook. And then when she landed on the set she'd taken before Heath had insulted her, she burst out laughing.

"What is it?" Sheila scooted to Camille's side and then hooted with laughter. "Oh my God, is that Heath? Why is Jason in Heath's crotch?"

It was an action shot, and Camille had somehow taken the photo so it looked like Jason had his face buried in

Heath's groin. Camille and Sheila looked at the photo at all angles until they were red in the face and almost coughing from laughing so hard. "This is the best thing I've ever seen," Camille said between giggles. She looked back at the photo, and the laughing fit started all over again.

Sheila gasped suddenly. "You have to publish this in the yearbook!"

"What? No. Mr. Andros would never allow it."

"So what! You can swap it out for another photo and he'll never know. I know you help design the pages and send it to the printer."

Camille bit her lip. The temptation was almost too strong: it would be a great revenge on Heath to publish this particular photo. Camille, though, wasn't as daring as Sheila, and she knew Heath would be humiliated if she included it.

"I don't know, what if I get in trouble?"

Sheila scoffed. "For what? Including a picture you took at a football game in the football team spread? Last time I checked, you don't get expelled for stuff like that."

"Yeah, but still."

"You're way too nice. Heath humiliated you today and you're worried about his feelings? Come on. He deserves this and worse."

Camille looked at the photo again. Sheila was right: Heath did deserve to be taken down a peg, and he'd had no right to talk to her like he had. Heath always acted like he was the greatest thing since sliced bread, and having people laugh at him would be a sweet kind of revenge. Plus, he'd never know for sure who had taken the photo or who'd put it in the yearbook.

"I'll do it," Camille said, emailing the photo to herself to make sure she had a copy of it. "I'll include it in the yearbook and Heath Dawson will wish he'd never been born."

1

10 years later…

"You're photographing *who*?"

Camille held her phone to her ear even as she kept packing. "The Savannah Bootleggers," she said, answering Sheila. "The team and the cheerleaders. It's for a benefit calendar. A couple of photoshoots in Savannah, a pre-season opener in South Carolina, then back to Savannah for one more game. Emma will be with Rich, and she's thrilled to spend the extra time with him before school starts again."

"She's not the only one thrilled. Holy shit, Camille! How did this happen?"

"One of the league's photographers quit unexpectedly and they're looking for his replacement. They kept my application from last year and decided to give me a shot. I'm taking this job as an independent consultant, but if they like what I do…"

"Oh my God, oh my God, that's awesome! But the Savannah Bootleggers? Heath Dawson's the team's wide receiver!"

Of course Sheila would bring him up right when she'd opened her underwear drawer. Now she was staring at a mix of practical cotton and silk and lace as images of Heath Dawson floated in her head. "I know his position and what team he plays for, Sheila. He's Emma's favorite player."

"Right," Sheila snorted. "Like that's the *only* reason you know what team he plays for. Because *your daughter* likes him. Not because he's twice as hot as he was in high school and thinking about him is the way you get off the hardest."

"I said that one night when I was tipsy."

Oh, how she wished she'd never told Sheila that little tidbit. Even more, she wished it had been any other team she'd been asked to photograph. It was a big opportunity for her, but her excitement about the job had been instantly tempered by the knowledge that the Bootleggers' wide receiver was none other than her arch nemesis Heath Dawson, the man who'd left Peachtree ten years ago for UCLA, then played for a team on the West Coast before joining the Bootleggers two years ago.

It had been bad enough that her daughter loved him, mostly because he did a ridiculous dance each time the team scored, which meant Camille had had to endure Emma never missing a game, Emma talking about him incessantly, and Emma putting up posters of him in her room.

Oh, the horror!

"Oh my God. You're going to finally sleep with him."

"What? Are you crazy! I haven't seen the guy in ten years and the last time we talked, he mistook me for a *boy*. Not to mention you always thought he was a jerk. Of course I'm not going to sleep with him." Hand hovering above her underwear, she finally grabbed several of her prettiest panties; not that anyone, let alone Heath Dawson, would be seeing them, but if she was going to faceoff with Heath at some point, she wanted to feel her most confident; not like the skinny tomboy he'd humiliated all those years ago. Of course, she didn't look anything like a skinny tomboy anymore, but inside, that's how she'd always feel, at least where Heath was concerned.

"Never say never," Sheila teased.

"Oh, I'm definitely saying never," Camille shot back. "Heath Dawson was a cocky jerk back then and from what I can tell from all the press he gets, he's still a cocky jerk today." Well, at least cocky; the press actually went out of its way to point out that even as the league's top wide receiver, Heath was extremely well-liked by everyone, especially the ladies.

"Who cares if he's all cock as long as he can do the walk. And he most definitely can. Besides, you say that now, but then you're going to get a good look at him, and he's going to get a good look at *you*, and... Lordy lordy, can I go with you?"

"Absolutely not."

"Fine. But I want details when you get back."

"There aren't going to be any details worth sharing. But I should go. Rich is picking up Emma in about an hour and I need to finish packing."

"Take something sexy!"

"Goodbye, Sheila. Love you!" Camille hung up the phone, then started folding blouses and pants into her suitcase. Should she take the white blouse or the purple? The white was boring but standard, but the purple brought out the green in her eyes...then again, they were both serviceable, straight-forward button-up shirts.

She decided on the purple just as her seven-year-old daughter Emma walked in and sat on the bed.

"Can you get his autograph for me?" she said, her face lit up with excitement. "You know he's my favorite!"

"I'll try, honey. But he's a busy guy."

Emma's bottom lip pushed forward, and Camille had to hide a smile. She looked so much like her ex that it was almost disconcerting. Camille sometimes wondered if Emma had gotten any genes from her or if she were just a clone of her father. Thankfully for everyone, Camille and Rich had split up fairly amicably (well, as amicably as possible given Rich had cheated on her), co-parenting Emma with only minimal bumps for two human beings trying to raise another, smaller human being. She had to admit the fact Rich spent plenty of time with Emma when he wasn't on the road had gone a long way toward healing old wounds.

Camille reached forward and poked that pouting,

bottom lip. "I told you I'd try. But you know I have work to do, so it's not going to be my number one goal, okay?"

"But you will *try?*"

Camille smiled wider—at least Emma got her stubbornness from her. "Yes, I'll try."

Emma squealed and began bouncing on the bed, but when her bouncing almost bounced the suitcase right off, Camille gave her daughter *The Look*. Emma was smart enough to know what that meant and settled down—as much as a seven-year-old could settle down at any given time—only bouncing lightly as Camille finished packing.

Unfortunately, she couldn't stop thinking about the last time she'd talked to Heath. She'd hidden it from Sheila, but now that she was going to come face-to-face with him after not seeing him for over a decade, she was a mixture of anxious and...excited? No, she told herself, rolling her panties and placing them neatly inside her suitcase. She just didn't want to have some awkward conversation about high school and yearbook photos and waterboys...

She cringed inside, telling herself that had been a long time ago. Still, it hadn't been so long that the memory didn't occasionally rear its ugly head and make her feel the humiliation all over again. At least she'd gotten her revenge.

After that horrible night, she'd avoided Heath for the rest of the school year. She'd taken great pains to make sure she never got within twenty feet of him, not caring if she wracked up tardy slips or detentions given they had math class together and classrooms close to one another for three other subjects. She consistently arrived late to math, heading directly to Sheila, who always saved her a seat on the other side of the room from where Heath sat. She stayed behind to talk to the teachers or took the long way to classes just to avoid him. Her grades had actually started to suffer as a result, but that hadn't stopped her.

She'd also gone through with her plan to publish that photo of Heath in the yearbook, Sheila egging her on. When Camille had first opened the printed yearbook and saw the photo, she'd laughed and laughed. And she'd laughed even more when the entire school laughed at football star Heath Dawson, nicknaming him and Jason "Crotch Buddies." To her surprise, Heath had taken it in stride, although she'd thought he'd looked at her with a small amount of anger more than once. Jason hadn't taken it as well and had tried to get the yearbook reprinted, but at that point, it was too late. Trevor, the student yearbook editor, had tried to find out who'd done it, but Camille had refused to spill. Just after the school's graduation ceremony, Camille had seen Heath walking toward her with a determined expression on his face, and she'd practically run away.

"Do you think his girlfriend will be there?" Emma had stopped bouncing and was now attempting to help Camille fold the rest of her clothes.

"Whose girlfriend?"

Emma huffed, like Camille was the dumbest person in existence. "Heath's! She's the blond cheerleader, you remember?"

Ah, right. The *latest* blond cheerleader who looked pretty much identical to the one Heath had been photographed with last month. And the one six months before that. Blond, tall, thin, built, and gorgeous. Certainly no one who could ever be mistaken for being a boy whether she was wearing an old jersey and jeans or not.

"Honey, I think all of the cheerleaders are blond." Camille went to the bathroom, rummaging around for her toiletries. She gathered everything she'd need—shampoo, face soap, lotion, contact solution—then placed her bag of toiletries on one side of the suitcase, her bag of makeup on the other. Should she bring her own hair dryer or would the hotel's work? She mulled it over, as her hair dryer could dry her long hair faster than most hair dryers. Then again, she'd probably put her hair up when she was working...

"Do you think he loves her?" Emma asked abruptly, with the guilelessness only small children possessed.

"Do you mean does Heath love his girlfriend?" Camille was about to give a noncommittal answer, but seeing the hope on Emma's face, Camille softened. "I'm sure he does, honey. He seems like a good man, despite the ridiculous dancing."

Lately, Emma had been asking if certain couples loved each other—did Bill and Sandra love each other? Did Tim and Felix love each other? Did Daddy love Michelle? Or Bettina? Or any of the other women he'd dated through the years—and Camille couldn't help but wonder if Emma were trying to figure out why her own parents didn't love each other anymore.

The thing was, Camille had never loved Rich and he hadn't loved her. They'd had fun together in the beginning, but Emma had been a surprise discovered the summer after their freshman year in college, just after Camille's father had died. He'd instantly offered to marry her, and she'd been too afraid to go it on her own to refuse. Somehow, with the help of Rich's parents, they'd managed to finish college, and she'd done her best to be a good mother and wife, one that supported Rich's dreams of being a professional hockey player. And even though Rich had attained his dream, the harsh reality of being married to a professional athlete who traveled so much had quickly led to the demise of their marriage. Rich's cheating hadn't devastated her, but it had taught her a painful lesson. Or rather, it had *reinforced* the lesson she should have taken to heart after her run in with Heath so long ago: she needed to resist her attraction to athletes and focus on herself.

Her career. And Emma. Those were the only things that mattered.

She zipped up her suitcase, glancing at the time. She had a half hour to kill before Rich picked up Emma. She spent the time chatting with her daughter and making sure she had everything she'd need for the week. When Rich arrived and parked his flashy sportscar at the curb, she waved to her ex, then hugged Emma tight and gave her a kiss. "See you next week, baby, but we'll talk every day.

Lots of birthday party planning to do. Have you thought more about a birthday party theme?"

"Still thinking. Bye, Mom. Have fun with Heath!" Emma said even as she skipped to meet her father. After they drove away, she stood on the front porch to get her bearings and give herself a little pep talk. She could do this. She could have fun.

Not *with* Heath Dawson but *in spite* of him.

She could take her photos and chances were he'd never know she was the waterboy who'd made his life hell during senior year.

Then she'd come home, collect her paycheck, land her dream job and hopefully never think about him again.

* * *

Two hours later, Camille arrived at South Beach on Tybee Island, about thirty minutes outside Downtown Savannah. As she watched, several members of the Savannah Bootleggers played an impromptu game on the sand, tossing a football back and forth as the cheerleaders watched.

"Going wide!" one of the shirtless men yelled— Camille recognized him as Kyle Young, the Bootleggers quarterback. He was the superstar of the team, featured on shows and magazine covers and even appearing in a movie or two. Kyle was tanned and muscular, and Camille couldn't help but appreciate his six-pack, even from yards away.

Heath was nowhere to be seen. She frowned, wondering if he had heard who was taking the photos and had bailed.

"You're the photographer?"

She looked up to see Alec LeBrun, tight end, jogging up to her. He was huge, shoulders broad and muscular, but his warm smile gave him a boyish air. According to the tabloids, he'd just gotten engaged to his gorgeous girlfriend a few weeks ago.

"Yep, that's me," she replied, gesturing to her camera hanging around her neck. "How'd you guess?"

Alec laughed, flashing bright white teeth.

"Okay, okay, let's get everyone together," a pretty redheaded woman yelled, her hair pulled into a tight bun.

"Heath's not here yet," Alec said.

The redhead smiled tightly and though she looked in Alec's direction, she seemed to focus on something over his shoulder rather than meet his gaze straight on. "No, Mr. Dawson has yet to grace us with his presence, but we wait for no man. Or woman." She turned to Camille, holding out her hand. She had the brightest blue eyes she'd ever seen. "I'm Ruby O'Brien, publicist and football player wrangler. I'll be keeping these lunatics in line today."

Camille glanced at Alec, who frowned before he turned away and rejoined the others. Turning back to Ruby, Camille shook the woman's hand, smiling at her no-nonsense approach. "Camille Pollert. Your help would be great." She was about to ask that they begin with groups of five, mixed gender, when she saw a man and woman walking up. The man was tall and tan and Camille could tell he was attractive even from a distance. But it was when she heard his voice that she realized who it was: Heath Dawson.

"Sorry I'm late, everybody! Traffic. You know the drill." He slapped his buddies on the shoulder, and they heckled him for his tardiness. The woman at his side—a tall, leggy blond, probably the same one Emma had been talking about—hung onto his arm like a barnacle. "Did I miss anything?" Heath asked.

Camille bit her lip, annoyance filling her. Leave it to Heath to be late and to interrupt her without even noticing she existed. He hadn't changed one bit since they were in high school. But as she watched him make his way to the group of people, she couldn't help but admit that some things *had* changed: he was more muscular, a five o'clock shadow on his cheeks and strong jaw. Teenage Heath had been handsome in a boyish kind of way; adult Heath was gorgeous in a rugged, overtly masculine kind of way that caused Camille to flush all over. Of course, she'd seen him on TV. Magazine covers. Emma's posters. But it had been easier to blow off his appeal when he wasn't standing in front of her, his smile as bright and wide as it had been when they'd been younger, but now enhanced with a spark of sensuality. Heath knew he affected women and he used that to his advantage.

Annoyed with herself for letting Heath affect her again even after all of these years, she called out, "Yes, I was just about to get people into groups." Looking at Heath, she added, "I'm glad you were finally able to join us."

Heath turned his attention to her, his eyebrows raised. Camille instantly felt over-exposed, and she cursed herself for her sharp tongue. The last thing she wanted was to draw attention to herself and possibly give Heath a reason to recognize her.

But how could he? She'd gained weight in all the right places and even some not so ideal ones since high school, mostly thanks to giving birth to Emma, and she'd learned to wrangle her dark hair so it was now long and glossy. She wore makeup and nice, feminine clothing, although nothing flashy.

Camille looked away from Heath, who seemed to be assessing her even more closely. "I'll be taking action shots at the game on Sunday, but right now we're going for a fun vibe. Happy. If everyone could get in groups of five, with three men and two women, that would be great," she said. The group hardly paid attention to her, though, and continued talking and laughing. Ruby was a few yards away now, talking on her phone.

About to call out her directions even more loudly, Camille was surprised when Heath cupped his mouth and shouted, "Hey, you assholes, quiet down and listen to the lovely lady here or I'll dump sand down all of your shorts!"

The group laughed and quieted down instantly, Camille couldn't help but be impressed. She stood back a bit and repeated her directions. Men grabbed women's wrists, a few play-fighting over a cheerleader, before they finally formed into suitable groups. A couple of groups had four men with one woman, but Camille could work with that.

"Okay, I'm going to start with this group, take a few photos, and move this way," Camille said as she pointed. "Remember, lots of laughter and smiles. No serious model poses or super sexy stuff either."

The guys guffawed, a few saying dirty things to some of the cheerleaders.

Camille fell into the zone, taking photos and directing people. She knew what she was doing here, with the camera in front of her face, the sound of the shutter and the play of bodies across the screen. She'd fallen in love with photography as a young girl, and she'd only gotten more talented in the intervening years. She freelanced because the flexible schedule gave her more time with Emma, but her daughter was in school and staying with Rich roughly half-time, which meant she had more time to devote to her career. She'd always wanted to photograph for the NFL and now that dream was so close she could practically taste it.

Several minutes later, she paused and reviewed what she had. Pleased with the shots she'd already gotten, she moved to the group with Heath in the middle.

"Okay, give me happy! Smiles and laughter, please!" She raised her camera, but she realized that Heath was staring at her again. When she caught his stare, he grinned.

"I'm feeling the need for some inspiration. Do you know any jokes?" Heath asked.

"I'm not really the type for jokes," Camille said shortly.

"That's too bad. You look like you could use some loosening up."

There he went, making his unsolicited observations again. She placed a hand on one hip. "I suppose you've got a bunch of jokes you're just dying to tell me?"

"I like to make the ladies laugh as much as the next guy."

She flashed him a tight smile, determined not to let him get to her, when what she really wanted to say was, *Yeah, but usually they're laughing at you, not with you.* Of course, that wouldn't be very professional of her, so she simply said, "Go for it."

More people laughed, although the leggy blond with Heath looked annoyed, pushing her bottom lip forward.

Heath held up his hands to quiet his friends. Then he studied Camille from head to toe, taking his time, making her flush, before he said, "How do football players do it?"

God, why had she challenged him? She could tell by the teasing glint in his eye, and the type of joke, that the punch line was going to be sexually charged, but she'd been around ribald football players long enough to know if she gave the slightest hint of being uptight, it would only go badly for her. "How?" she asked gamely.

"For over two hours in eleven different positions."

Delighted in spite of herself, Camille had to fight hard

not to laugh. Instead, she shook her head, as if he exasperated her, and waved a hand. "Okay, now that that's out of the way, can you guys give me the shots I need, please?"

"You deliberately didn't laugh."

Camille took a picture of him, liking the way he frowned when she ignored him.

When she kept snapping pictures, he approached her and held his hand up in front of the lens.

"Come on, admit it. You thought it was funny."

Camille sighed. He hadn't even given her the time of day years before, and now he couldn't stop flirting. Why? Because she was so different from his blond cheerleaders? Because she represented a challenge? That had to be it. But she'd teach him that even sexy football players didn't win every challenge. "The only thing I'll admit is you like to hear yourself talk too much. I'm surprised you can stop doing it long enough to score."

They were having a good old-fashioned showdown, and many of the other football players and cheerleaders had gathered around them. Kyle Young whooped and congratulated Camille for her putdown. Then Alec shouted out, "Looks like you're definitely not scoring today, Dawson!"

Heath, though, wasn't one to let up that easily. "How's about we bet on that?"

Camille frowned. He just wanted to get a rise out of her. And he was: her nipples prickled with his words and she had the stupidest desire to let him touch her all over.

She'd never felt like this with any guy—not even her ex-husband—and she still didn't understand the hold Heath had over her.

"Here's a bet," Camille finally replied. "I bet you can't keep your mouth shut for an entire hour. If I win, you have to be quiet for the rest of the day."

"And if I win?"

"It won't matter, since you won't be able to do it." Of course he wouldn't, Camille thought, truly convinced. The guy was a total attention hound.

"But *if* I win?"

"You get whatever you want."

Camille instantly regretted her words, especially as the girls tittered. Heath's eyebrows rose, and his gaze landed on her breasts before moving to her lips. Then he moved closer to speak in her ear. "I get a kiss," he finally said slowly, and surprise and heat filled every inch of Camille in equal measure. It was the last thing she'd been expecting him to say given the tall blond that had been hanging all over him. Wasn't she his girlfriend? Could he be that much of an asshole?

She glanced at the blond, who was glaring daggers at her. "But—"

"Genevieve likes to flirt with me, but we're not together, so you can't use her as an excuse. So as I was saying, I get a kiss whenever I want," he clarified. "Or does that scare you too much?"

Camille felt stupid for falling into his trap. She wanted to backtrack. Tell him absolutely not. But everyone was staring at them, and she just couldn't give him the satisfaction of surrendering. "Fine. It's a deal." She knew she sounded snappish, but Heath never failed to get a rise out of her, even a decade later.

Heath fell silent and she continued the photoshoot. She counted the minutes, glancing at her watch every so often, and each time she did, Heath looked at her with a "Did you think I couldn't do it?" kind of look. Camille just glared at him as she moved onto the next group.

The minutes passed, and she kept tabs on Heath throughout, to see if he were, indeed, keeping their bet. He remained silent, not even laughing, not even talking when the leggy blond whined at him to say something. Camille had to admit that the man was stubborn.

After finishing up over an hour later, Camille realized that Heath had won. Flustered, thinking about him kissing her, she began fingering her hair while looking through the photos.

Heath stepped up to her, and Camille's heart pounded. Would he claim the kiss now, in front of everyone? Lowering her camera with shaky hands, Camille was about to ask him what was up, when he said in both amusement and surprise, "Is that you, Waterboy?"

BOOKS BY VIRNA

KISS TALENT AGENCY
Book 1: Lip Action (Simon)
Book 2: Locking Lips (Caleb)

THE BEDDING THE BACHELORS
Book 1: Bedding The Wrong Brother (Rhys)
Book 2: Bedding The Bad Boy (Max)
Book 3: Bedding The Billionaire (Jamie)
Book 4: Bedding The Best Friend (Ryan)
Book 5: Bedding The Biker Next Door (Cole)
Book 6: Bedding The Bodyguard (Luke)
Book 7: Bedding The Best Man (Gabe)
Book 8: Bedding The Boss (Eric)
Book 9: Bedding The Baby Daddy (Dante)

HOME TO GREEN VALLEY
Book 1: What Love Can Do (Quinn)
Book 2: The Way Love Goes (Conor)
Book 3: I'm Gonna Love You (Brady)
Book 4: Best Of My Love (Riley)
Book 5: Because You Love Me (Sean)

HARD AS NAILS
Book 1: Hard Time (Street)
Book 2: Hard Case (Slate)
Book 3: Hard Core (Axel)
Book 4: Hard Place (Jericho)
Book 5: Hard Act (Davis)**

GOING DEEP
Book 1: Down Deep (Heath)
Book 2: Royally Deep (Kyle)

SAY YOU LOVE ME
Book 1: Say It Sexy
Book 2: Say It Sweet

ROCK CANDY
Book 1: Rock Strong
Book 2: Rock Dirty
Book 3: Rock Wild

PARA-OPS PARANORMAL ROMANTIC SUSPENSE
Book 1: Knox: Chosen by Blood
Book 2: Wraith: Chosen by Fate
Book 3: Dex: Chosen by Sin

**Coming Soon

ABOUT THE AUTHOR

Virna DePaul is a *New York Times* and *USA Today* bestselling author of steamy, suspenseful fiction. Whether it's vampires, a Para-Ops team, hot cops or swoon-worthy identical twin brothers, her stories center around complex individuals willing to overcome incredible odds for love. Bedding The Wrong Brother, which begins the Bedding The Bachelors Series, is a #1 Bestselling Contemporary Romance and a USA Today Bestseller.

Virna loves to hear from readers at www.virnadepaul.com.

CONTACT VIRNA HERE
Website: www.virnadepaul.com
Twitter: @virnadepaul
Email: virna@virnadepaul.com